**'Where do w...**
**Richard mur...**

'To bed,' Nicola s...
chest.

'That's fine by me.'

She pushed him away more vigorously. 'That's not what I meant at all!'

'It wasn't?' There was laughter in his voice.

There had been nothing tentative about his first kiss. Now, as he kissed her for the second time, she knew it would be futile to pretend she didn't want him.

**Dear Reader**

In February, we celebrate one of the most romantic times of the year—St Valentine's Day, when messages of true love are exchanged. At Mills & Boon we feel that our novels carry the Valentine spirit on throughout the year and we hope that readers agree. Dipping into the pages of our books will give you a taste of true romance every month...so chase away those winter blues and look forward to spring with Mills & Boon!

Till next month,

*The Editor*

**Anne Weale** was still at school when a women's magazine published some of her stories. At twenty-five she had her first novel accepted by Mills & Boon. Now, with a grown-up son and still happily married to her first love, Anne divides her life between her winter home, a Spanish village ringed by mountains and vineyards, and a summer place in Guernsey, one of the many islands around the world she has used as backgrounds for her books.

**Recent titles by the same author:**

THE FABERGÉ CAT

# TURKISH DELIGHTS

BY

## ANNE WEALE

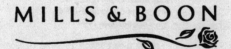

MILLS & BOON LIMITED
ETON HOUSE, 18-24 PARADISE ROAD
RICHMOND, SURREY TW9 1SR

For Angela, Katrina, Sara, Sheila and Valerie who
shared the journey which inspired this story. Also for
Ayhan, our guide, whose courtesy, patience and
humour smoothed the way. And for M, the world's
best travelling companion.

*First published in Great Britain 1993*
*by Mills & Boon Limited*

© Anne Weale 1993

*Australian copyright 1993*
*Philippine copyright 1994*
*This edition 1994*

ISBN 0 263 78310 3

*Set in Times Roman 10 on 10½ pt.*
*91-9402-58286 C*

*Made and printed in Great Britain*

# CHAPTER ONE

FOR Nicola Temple, one of the delights of living in London was to walk down a street where, between 1851 and 1860, Charles Dickens had lived and written *Bleak House*. Or through a nearby square where, in a house destroyed by bombing in 1941, Virginia Woolf had written some of her novels.

Nicola's parents lived in the country, but close enough to London for her to commute from their home. But, once established as a junior editor, she had wanted to be independent; to enjoy the pleasures of city life rather than merely working there from nine to five.

Not that she had a nine-to-five job. Being a publisher's editor was a vocation rather than merely a means of earning her living, especially now she was a commissioning editor with her own list of authors.

One of them was coming to lunch with her today at the Café des Amis du Vin, a bistro near Covent Garden. Her expenses allowance didn't run to the elegant restaurants where the senior editorial staff entertained the best-selling authors on the Barking & Dollis list. But as this author was a suburban housewife who had written her first novel at the kitchen table while her toddler and baby were having their afternoon nap, lunch at any London restaurant was a rare treat for her.

One day in the future, Nicola hoped, they would both reach the heights of lunching at the Savoy. Her own target was a seat on the board of B & D's directors, and she felt sure that, with her encouragement, some of her authors had it in them to become famous best-sellers.

Most of the editorial staff lived on the outskirts of London and didn't arrive at the office until ten. Nicola liked to be at her desk at nine in order to have a quiet hour before her telephone started to ring.

Many of the calls were internal, but sometimes her authors would ring up out of the blue and expect her to switch her mind to their problems; often their personal hang-ups as well as professional difficulties.

The reception area at Barking & Dollis was staffed by two girls: one at the switchboard dealing with almost non-stop calls and the other receiving packages brought in by motorbike messengers and directing visitors to offices on other floors. This morning an arty-looking young man with a large portfolio, probably containing roughs for a book jacket, was perched on one of the leather sofas.

Smiling at all three, Nicola said, 'Morning, Polly. Morning, Fiona.'

Aware of them eyeing her new suit—usually she came to work in a sweater and skirt—she ran up the stairs to Editorial on the second floor.

Here the whole floor was divided into glass-walled cubicles, their size depending on the status of their occupants. Later in the day the most noticeable feature of the area would be the blue screens of the computer terminals used by the secretaries and also by the editorial staff when they wanted to check the details of a contract or the current sales figures of a particular title.

At the moment the screens were blank and Nicola had the place to herself.

The first of her colleagues to arrive was Gordon, who was in charge of the crime fiction list.

'Morning, Nicola. Ready for a coffee?' The coffee machine was always his first port of call.

'Yes, please, Gordon.'

A few moments later he came back with two polystyrene beakers.

'I hear the New Broom is in town. Any day now the clean sweep will start.'

He was talking about Richard Russell, whose photograph had been in both the American and British publishing periodicals when his appointment as chief executive of Barking & Dollis was announced.

Although he had already made one or two flying visits to the firm now under his control, Nicola had been out of the office on the day he had toured the building and met the editorial staff.

There had been much speculation in the trade papers about the measures Russell would take to pull the firm out of its serious financial difficulties.

'What do *you* think he'll do?' she asked Gordon.

'Something fairly drastic, that's for sure. Neither of us has much to worry about. We pull our weight. But I——' Gordon broke off. 'That sounds like my telephone. See you...'

Watching him hurry to his office, one wall of it massed with books, including titles by several of the most popular names in crime fiction, Nicola knew he had little to fear from the man he called the New Broom. Two of Gordon's most successful authors had clauses written into their contracts ensuring that if he left Barking & Dollis they would be free to follow him. That alone was a powerful insurance. No firm, in difficult times, wanted to lose writers whose new books always reached high ratings on the best-seller lists and stayed there for many weeks.

None of the books on her own list had ever done that. But at least one of her authors had the potential to best-sell in a few years' time. So, although a great many people in publishing had lost their jobs in the past few months, Nicola wasn't too worried about her own position.

When, that afternoon, she returned to the office after lunching with her author, there was a note on her desk.

Please call Mr Russell's secretary immediately.

She picked up the internal telephone and tapped the extension number.

'This is Nicola Temple. You wanted to speak to me?'

'Mr Russell wants to see you. He's busy at the moment. I'll call you when he's free.'

Nicola checked her hair and make-up. Then she tried to get on with some work. But it was difficult to concentrate with a summons to see the chief executive looming over her.

What did he want? Merely to give her the once-over?

She was kept in suspense for only ten minutes before his secretary rang back.

'Mr Russell will see you now.'

The CE's suite was on the top floor, with the door to his secretary's office immediately opposite the lift. To the left was the boardroom, to the right a conference room.

Nicola had been on this floor only once before, for her interview with the previous CE. The same pleasant-faced, fortysomething secretary was working at a desk near the door to the inner sanctum.

Receiving a 'go ahead' nod, Nicola tapped on the door and heard a brisk voice say, 'Come in.'

A friendly smile already forming round her mouth, she turned the handle and entered.

The new chief executive was using a notebook computer of the kind she longed to own but at present couldn't afford.

For a few moments longer his fingers moved lightly over the keys. Then he stopped work and stood up. She had heard he was tall, but hadn't realised how tall. As she walked towards him, he subjected her to a scrutiny which seemed to leave no detail of her appearance unregistered. And it wasn't a friendly inspection. He didn't smile as she approached.

She had never felt her self-possession more severely tested than in the first moments of being appraised by Richard Russell's critical blue eyes.

Without shaking hands, he said, 'Sit down, Miss Temple. I wanted to see you earlier but you weren't in. Where were you?'

'Having lunch with an author.'

One of his straight black eyebrows rose into an inverted tick.

'A long lunch,' he said drily. 'You were out of the office until nearly four o'clock.'

'We had a lot to discuss. Actually we left the restaurant at three, but hadn't finished our talk so I walked to her station with her.'

'What was the purpose of this prolonged discussion? What did it achieve?' he asked.

The questions were hard to answer in the precise, quick-fire way she felt he expected.

'We talked about a lot of things... I think Margaret went home feeling encouraged and stimulated. She doesn't get much support from her husband and——'

'Long lunches are an expensive waste of time which I intend to curtail if not to ban altogether,' he cut in incisively. 'This company is in trouble, Miss Temple... or do you prefer "Ms" Temple?'

There were women on the staff who would have been infuriated by the sarcastic tone of this query and its implications. Clearly he was an arch anti-feminist and liked everyone to know it.

Well, he was the boss, and it was his privilege to impose his views on his employees if he chose. Whether, in so doing, he would get the best out of them was another matter. But that wasn't her concern. Her priority was to please him and clearly, by being absent when he sent for her, she had got off on the wrong foot.

'I answer to either,' she said pleasantly. 'Or to my first name, Nicola, if you prefer.'

'This company is in trouble,' he repeated. 'It has been for some time. Because the previous administration failed to take steps to stop the rot, there is now no option but to make stringent... extremely stringent cut-backs.'

In the harsh set of his mouth as he paused, and in the stern blue gaze fixed on her face, Nicola read signs that made her mouth and throat go dry.

'I have here——' he tapped the casing of the compact computer '—all Barking & Dollis's records since—far too late, in my view—the company started to make use of modern technology. I've spent the past two weeks studying the records of every member of staff and the profitability of every title published by B & D during the past several years. Now it's my unpleasant task to do what should have been done long ago.'

Again he paused, the merciless stare fixed on her face. She knew that at any moment he would deliver a verdict against which there would be no appeal.

'The books you have commissioned since your promotion have not performed well enough to justify their place on our list. I'm sorry to have to tell you your services are no longer required.'

Even though she had already guessed what was coming, Nicola still couldn't believe he had dismissed her.

After some moments of silence, she managed to say unsteadily, 'You mean... I'm sacked... just like that.'

He nodded. 'I'd prefer you to leave at once... this afternoon. There's nothing to be gained by the staff who are leaving remaining here under notice. It's better they start job-hunting immediately.'

'I—I can't believe this,' she stammered. 'I can't believe that after three and a half years I'm being chucked out without notice. I'm not a slacker, Mr Russell. I've put in nearly as many hours in my own time as in the firm's time. And what's going to happen to my authors? Are you going to ditch them too?'

'If I had been heading this company, most of them wouldn't have been taken on,' he said curtly. 'We'll fulfil our contractual obligations but, where there is only an option to publish the next book, most of your authors will have to look elsewhere. It's tough, I know. But it's the nature of business...and publishing is a business. Not, as it once was, "an occupation for gentlemen"...or for young ladies with literary inclinations.'

'That isn't fair,' she protested. 'It may apply to a handful of the women in publishing, but it certainly doesn't to me. I'm not subsidised by rich parents...or filling in time till I marry. I see my job as a career.'

'It's no use arguing, Miss Temple. I didn't arrive at this decision without careful thought. Staff cuts are unavoidable. You would agree, wouldn't you, that as a young single woman you're in a better position to survive redundancy than a man with a wife and children to support?'

That silenced her for a moment. Then she said, 'In most cases yes, but for all you know I may be the sole supporter of an elderly parent. Many single women are.'

'I have your background notes here.'

He touched a couple of keys and swivelled the computer towards her. On the screen she saw her original CV followed by a heading 'Editorial Director's Report'. The screen wasn't large enough to show this unless Richard Russell used the scroll key. Instead he turned the screen back towards him.

Then, reading from another section of the file on her, he said, 'You spend Monday to Friday in London and most weekends at your parents' home in Kent. Your father is a branch manager for one of the major insurance companies. Your mother is secretary of a gardeners' circle and an active supporter of several local charities. You have no one dependent on you.'

'Except myself. My parents can't afford to keep me. And with all the so-called "rationalisations" there've been in publishing recently, there are more people out of work than posts to be filled. I've no hope of getting another job.'

He didn't deny it, but said calmly, 'In publishing, possibly not...at least in the immediate future. The present recession won't last forever. They never do.

Meanwhile, you have skills applicable to other occupations. Your father may be able to pull some strings for you.'

'I don't want another occupation...and I don't believe I deserve to be thrown out of this one. I can't deny that none of the books I've handled has done very brilliantly, but they haven't been disasters either. It takes time to build an author.'

'I've dipped into the books you've bought for us, Miss Temple, and they strike me as mainly reading for people such as your mother...middle-class, middle-aged housewives.'

'There are a lot of them about, Mr Russell,' she retorted. 'They——'

He cut in, 'I'm afraid I haven't time to discuss the public's reading habits. I'm too busy addressing the problem of how to save this company from going into liquidation.' He rose to his feet.

'The blame for your predicament doesn't lie with me. Your understandable ire should be aimed at the previous management who failed to foresee and prepare for the changes affecting the book industry. I'm sorry we can't continue to employ you, but I also think, from your record, that you may find yourself more comfortable in a different kind of occupation. Publishing—like the theatre and the movies—has a misleading glamour about it.'

He came round the desk and moved in the direction of the door.

'In New York, we've already had to trim our sails to the rough winds of recession. It's going to get equally tough over here. You have many excellent qualities to help you relocate and those will be emphasised in the reference which I'll sign later today and you'll receive tomorrow.' He opened the door and held out his hand. 'I wish you luck, Miss Temple.'

It was an automatic reflex to shake the hand he offered. For a moment she had the strange feeling that a

powerful current of energy was actually flowing through
the large firm hand enclosing her shaky one. Then the
contact was broken and he was waiting for her to go.

'Goodbye.' She could feel his impatience to get on.

'Goodbye.' To her surprise, her reply sounded normal.
But inside she was starting to fall apart.

His secretary said, 'You'd better sit down for a minute.'
She produced a beaker of water. 'Sip this. If it's any
comfort, you're not the only one,' she went on sym-
pathetically. 'A lot of desks are being cleared this
afternoon.'

It took time for the words to sink in. Nicola felt dazed,
as if she had just cracked her head on something hard.

After some moments, she said, 'Who are the others?'

'Three in Editorial, two in Publicity, one in Rights
and six from other departments...twelve altogether. It's
the biggest shake-up I remember and I've been here for
sixteen years. Maybe I'll be in the next tumbril. He may
import an American secretary...or replace me with a
robot. He's the first boss I've ever had who can type.
He types faster than I do, would you believe? His computer taught him!'

A small gadget attached to the front of her businesslike
blouse began to bleep.

'I'll have to go. He doesn't like to be kept waiting.'
With a kindly pat on Nicola's shoulder, she went to
answer the summons.


Terminal One was full of people with skis balanced on
their luggage trolleys when Nicola arrived at Heathrow
Airport soon after six a.m. on the last Saturday in
January.

Joining the line at the All Destinations check-in desk,
she kept a lookout for anyone else with luggage like hers:
a large dark green canvas grip with 'Amazing
Adventures' stencilled in fluorescent pink letters on the
side of it.

When her luggage had been weighed and tagged, she slung the rucksack containing her camera and other valuables over her shoulder by one strap and went through the security barrier and Passport Control to the main departure lounge.

Her passport, issued nine years ago, was almost due for renewal. But there wasn't a lot of difference between the photograph of her at seventeen and the way she looked this morning, without make-up, her thick, fair shoulder-length hair tied back at the nape of her neck.

At seventeen she had looked mature for her age, the type of kind, sensible girl who might take up nursing or teaching or become an invaluable secretary. Not, at that age, a pretty girl, although a discriminating eye might have seen the promise of something more lasting than prettiness.

Today, casually dressed and with her clear skin bare of anything but moisturiser, she looked younger than twenty-six. The traumas of three years ago hadn't left any visible scars.

Flight BA 676 to Istanbul was called just before eight. Most of the people who assembled in the final departure area were Turkish businessmen in dark overcoats with briefcases.

But a few passengers were dressed like Nicola in walking boots, jeans, sweatshirts and padded jackets. Hers, dark blue and filled with down, was on loan from her brother.

She was idly watching the last comers having their tickets checked when suddenly her dark grey eyes widened in startled dismay.

The tall man striding into view was someone she had seen before. Only once, a long time ago, but his features were imprinted on her memory as clearly as if it were yesterday.

This was the man who, for a while, had wrecked her life—and with as little compunction as if he were stepping on an ant or swatting a house fly.

The last time she had seen him, on that unforgettable day in the chief executive's office on the top floor of the Barking & Dollis building, he had been in the clothes of a high-powered international businessman.

Today he was wearing a military-style khaki sweater with cotton reinforcements at the shoulders and elbows and a pair of the multi-pocketed Rohan trousers her brother always wore on his expeditions.

His clothing left her in little doubt that he was also a member of the Amazing Adventures group. The realisation that, of all people, Richard Russell was going to be one of her travelling companions for the next sixteen days filled her with horror.

He had no right to be here, she thought angrily. A man with his means should be jetting off to one of the ritzy winter-sun resorts where tycoons and their women foregathered at this time of year, not butting in on a holiday designed for low-budget travellers who didn't mind roughing it.

Unaware of her hostile gaze fixed on his autocratic profile, Richard Russell strolled towards the doors through which very soon everyone in the waiting area would be despatched to their aircraft.

He appeared to have timed his arrival to suit his own convenience, ignoring the instruction to be there two hours before take-off.

Not bothering to take a seat, he stood near the doorway and inspected his fellow passengers. Before his survey reached Nicola, the doors were opened and people began to go through.

The interior of the plane was divided into two sections, the more expensive seats at the front being occupied by some of the businessmen and one elegant woman. The Euro-Traveller section at the rear was where Nicola and her as yet unknown fellow trekkers would be sitting.

Richard Russell was stowing his belongings in an overhead locker when she moved hurriedly past him, her face averted. At least she had been spared the ordeal of sitting next to the man and had a few hours to steel herself before being forced to shake hands with him.

As yet unheated, the aircraft felt cold. But it was nervous tension rather than the low temperature which made Nicola shiver as she fastened her seatbelt. Seeing Richard Russell had brought back all the wretchedness of the months after he had sacked her. And although the job she had now was as well paid and reasonably congenial, it didn't have the same prospects as the one she had lost, nor was the work as satisfying.

She had survived. She was still independent and solvent. But she wasn't as happy and fulfilled as she had been before her abrupt and arbitrary dismissal.

Presently, looking out of the window, she saw that they were flying over what looked like a fantasy world of jagged mountains and vast frozen lakes. Actually the lakes were the smooth surface of clouds and the fairytale mountains were the peaks of the central European alps.

For a while the excitement of being whisked across Europe to what had once been Constantinople, heart of the legendary Ottoman Empire, city of Suleiman the Magnificent, made her forget the occupant of a seat several rows in front of her.

But thinking about some of the other rulers of Constantinople, and their cruelty towards their inferiors, triggered thoughts of Richard Russell: the man who had cut short her career in publishing, and that of eleven of her colleagues, as ruthlessly as Sultan Mehmed the Conqueror had ordered the drowning of seven of his dead father's concubines.

What Richard Russell had done on the day described in the trade Press as 'one of the blackest dates in the history of British publishing' might not be as brutal a crime as ordering the execution of unwanted slave girls. But she had no doubt that, had he lived in those times, he would have been capable of equally merciless treatment of those in his power.

* * *

At Istanbul airport, Nicola was among the last to have
her passport checked. By the time she passed through
the barrier to the baggage reclaim area, most of the other
passengers had collected their luggage and were heading
in the direction of the Customs desks.

To her relief there was no sign of Richard Russell. It
seemed she had been mistaken and he wasn't one of her
group after all. Well, a fortnight staying in cheap
*pansiyons* was certainly not the sort of holiday she would
have expected him to choose from all she had heard and
read about him.

His father was an American senator, his grandfather
a multimillionaire whose possessions had included one
of the USA's most important publishing houses.

On his mother's side he was descended from British
aristocrats and, at his mother's insistence, had been educated at Eton like all his maternal forebears. On both
sides of the Atlantic he sprang from the most élite strata
of Anglo-American society. It was hardly likely that he
would choose to fraternise with the kinds of holiday-
makers who shopped around for bargain breaks and were
prepared to put up with some privations in order to see
the world.

Why he should have been flying Euro-Traveller instead of Business Class was a puzzle. But no doubt by
now he was on his way to the famous Pera Palas Hotel
or the modern luxury of the Sheraton where the kind of
people he was used to mixing with would stay.

Feeling better, Nicola cast a surreptitious eye over the
people who were going to be her travelling companions.
Not that she really minded what they were like as long
as he wasn't one of them.

When they had been through Customs and emerged
into the concourse, they were met by a smiling dark-eyed
girl with a cloud of curly black hair who suggested that,
before leaving the airport, they might like to go to the
bank at the far end of the concourse.

'You can leave your luggage here with me. I'll watch it for you.'

As they followed her directions, Nicola noticed that compared with the number of men in the building there were very few women about. Unaccustomed to being the cynosure of so many masculine eyes—particularly when she was dressed for trekking and deliberately had left off her normal make-up—she found it a little uncomfortable to be stared at so openly.

But she forgot about the stares when she saw who was standing at the cashier's window at the airport bank. Richard Russell. And on the floor by his feet was an Amazing Adventures bag.

He was one of the group after all.

When the kitbags had been stowed in the hold of the coach taking them to their overnight accommodation, and everyone was settled in their seats, the Turkish girl picked up a microphone.

'Good afternoon, ladies and gentlemen. My name is Nuray. I'm your tour guide. Your hotel is in the old part of the city near the Grand Bazaar and the famous Blue Mosque.'

As she listened, Nicola was aware of the presence of her *bête noire* two seats in front of her on the opposite side of the aisle. From where she sat, all she could see was one of Richard Russell's long legs stretched out in the aisle, part of a broad shoulder and the taut line of his cheekbone and jaw. His hair was as almost as dark as Nuray's and, judging by the colour of his skin, it wasn't long since he had spent time in the sun, possibly at Christmas. He had been lightly tanned, she recalled, the first time she'd met him.

So far he hadn't noticed her. Probably when he did he wouldn't remember her. Why should he? She had been in his presence for less than ten minutes, and she hadn't been the only person he had axed that day.

'The outskirts of large cities are never very prepossessing, are they?' said the woman sitting beside her. 'I'm Hilary Goodge.'

It was hard to judge how old she was because, although her hair was white, her skin wasn't lined except round her friendly hazel eyes. Also she looked very fit. A quick glance showed no ring on her wedding finger.

When Nicola had introduced herself, Miss Goodge said, 'Is this your first visit to Turkey?'

'Yes.'

'Mine too, although not my first "amazing adventure". Last year I trekked in Nepal.'

'That must have been very exciting.'

Miss Goodge nodded. 'Very. Have you travelled with AA before?'

'No, but my brother has. He's done their Peru trek.'

It was after four, local time, when they reached the hotel. As they climbed down from the coach, two small barefoot children appeared, silently begging for money with gestures indicating hunger.

Their signals tore at Nicola's heart. At present she had nothing in her wallet except large-denomination notes and was obliged to ignore them, like everyone else. But the sight of their muddy little feet, purple with cold, distressed her very much.

'They probably make a good thing out of stationing themselves outside a hotel frequented by first-world tourists,' said a cynical voice from behind her. A voice she would have recognised anywhere because of its distinctive timbre and its accent, a blend of Harvard and Oxford.

Turning, her grey eyes blazing, she said, 'That's the most heartless statement I've ever heard. How would *you* like to have bare feet on a raw day like this?'

# CHAPTER TWO

AS HER angry tone caught the attention of other members of the group, Richard Russell said calmly, 'I shouldn't.'

He handed the children the money he had been about to give them when she'd flared at him.

'But actions speak louder than words,' he added drily, cocking a quizzical eyebrow at her.

He moved away to remove his kitbag from the luggage hold.

Although she hadn't expected him to recognise her, it was curiously galling to be looked at without recognition by someone who had had such a catastrophic effect on her life.

Led by the Turkish girl, they carried their kitbags into the hotel. With marble floors, chandeliers and red and gold décor, the reception area and open-plan lounge were more luxurious than Nicola had expected.

But ten minutes later, looking out of the window in the twin-bedded room on the sixth floor she was sharing with Miss Goodge, she saw that the back of the hotel overlooked flats no better than slums. Quickly she let the net curtain fall into place, at the same time remembering Richard Russell's sardonic reply to her accusation of heartlessness.

'As Nuray says the tap water in Istanbul is heavily chlorinated, I'm going out to stretch my legs and buy some bottled water,' said Miss Goodge. 'If you go out, leave our key at the desk.'

Nicola nodded. 'I'll have a shower. Hot showers may be hard to come by later on. The brochure did warn us that on parts of the trek the facilities will be primitive.'

'That won't worry me,' said Miss Goodge. 'But some of the others may not care for it. It's too soon to form firm opinions, but I shouldn't be surprised if the tall man with blue eyes is the only member of the party who will take everything in his stride. He looks a very tough cookie.'

'What makes you think that?' asked Nicola.

'He reminds me of an explorer who gave a talk to the school where I used to teach. This man has the same fine-tempered look about him. You know how the metal for swords was repeatedly heated and cooled to improve its hardness and elasticity? Life puts some people through a similar process...makes them more resilient than most of us.'

Left on her own, Nicola pondered Miss Goodge's first impression of Richard Russell. To give the devil his due, he had rescued the publishing firm from the brink of insolvency. But had it been necessary to employ such Draconian methods?

One of the salesmen sacked at the same time as Nicola had had a nervous breakdown from which he would probably never recover fully. She had met him in the street not long ago and been shocked to hear that he was still out of work and unlikely ever to recover the standard of life he had lost when Richard made him redundant.

Presently she went down to the lobby to order coffee.

'Turkish or Nescafé?' the waiter asked.

'Turkish, please.'

'Make that two, will you? You don't mind if I join you, I hope?' said a man who had been on the coach.

'Not at all,' she said politely, although there was something about him she didn't take to. His hair was combed forward, probably to disguise a receding hairline, and his sweater was a colour she disliked.

'I'm Philip Shadwell.'

'Nicola Temple.' To be friendly, she asked, 'Have you trekked before?'

He shook his head. 'I haven't had a holiday for some time. The firm I worked for—an estate agency—went bust. But I'm on my feet again now.'

Their order arrived: tall glasses of water and small glasses of black coffee with a bowl of sugar cubes.

A few minutes later they were joined by two other members of the group, a brunette in her thirties and a much younger girl with red hair. They introduced themselves as Janet Sloane and Sylvie Bond.

At the airport Nicola had noticed Janet was much better dressed than everyone else in an expensive tweed jacket over what looked like a cashmere sweater with needlecord trousers and highly polished boots. She was also wearing a lot of make-up and her nails were varnished the same deep red as her sweater.

'What's the coffee like?' Janet asked, as the waiter reappeared.

Nicola sipped it. 'Very strong.'

Janet ordered a half-bottle of white wine and Sylvie enquired about soft drinks. She had a very fair skin and, as she talked to the waiter, who was also young and looking admiringly at her, she blushed.

'I'm surprised our guide is a woman,' said Janet. 'In a Muslim country I thought we'd be led by a man.'

They were sitting not far from the lift which had just reached lobby level. As a uniformed bellboy opened the door, Richard Russell stepped out.

Although he noticed the group sitting in the lounge, he didn't stroll over to join them, With a casual wave, he made for the doors.

Nicola noticed Janet's eyes following him down the marble steps to street level. She's welcome to him, she thought.

They had dinner at a kebab house. A table for twelve had been prepared for them and Nuray sat at one end and explained the menu.

Nicola sat between Miss Goodge and Philip with Janet and Richard opposite.

'Turkish cooking is supposed to be one of the three finest cuisines in the world, but somehow I don't think this is the place to sample it at its best,' said Janet, with a critical glance round the crowded restaurant.

'This isn't supposed to be a luxury holiday,' said Miss Goodge.

For her first course Nicola chose *piaz*, a dish of hard-boiled eggs and thinly sliced tomatoes on a bed of haricot beans.

Presently, after no one had spoken for some minutes, Nicola's room-mate said in slightly raised voice, 'Shall we introduce ourselves? I'm Hilary Goodge, retired schoolmistress. My main interest now is gardening.' She looked expectantly at Janet, who was facing her. 'And you are?'

'Janet Sloane... director of a management consultancy. I don't have time for many interests outside my work, which is very demanding.'

Smiling at him, Janet passed the cue for a thumbnail CV to Richard.

He said, 'Richard Russell. I work for a UK subsidiary of an American multi-media corporation. My other interests are rock-climbing, history and architecture.'

It was a modest way of describing the chairmanship of one of the oldest and most famous publishing houses in England, thought Nicola, as he looked across the table at her.

'I'm Nicola Temple. I'm secretary to the manager of a bookshop. My interests are reading and cooking,' she volunteered.

When everyone in the group had given brief details of themselves, Miss Goodge leaned forward to address their guide.

'How is it you speak such perfect English?'

'Thank you,' said Nuray, smiling. 'I don't think my English is perfect, but the reason I speak it quite well is because one of my sisters is married to an Englishman. I've spent many holidays with them since their wedding when I was eight and my sister was twenty. We're a large family. She is the eldest and I am the youngest. I still live with my parents in another part of Istanbul.'

At the end of the meal she told them each what they owed. The food was very cheap by English standards.

'I'd have preferred to pay more for something better, wouldn't you?' Janet murmured to Richard, taking some Turkish notes from an expensive wallet.

Nicola who, like some of the others, was keeping her money in a kangaroo-bag on a belt round her waist, saw him shrug and say, 'Mine wasn't bad. It filled the gap.'

She wondered what had brought Janet on this trip. A fortnight lazing in the sun by day and dancing under the stars by night at a glitzy resort in the Caribbean seemed more her style.

In the hotel lobby Nuray said, 'I'll be here at ten o'clock tomorrow to show you the Blue Mosque and other places of interest before we board the train for tomorrow night's journey. I hope you sleep well. Goodnight.'

When she had gone, someone suggested having a drink in the lounge, a proposal which met with approval from most of the group.

Miss Goodge said to Nicola, 'I had a late night last night. But there's no reason why you shouldn't stay up as long as you like. You won't disturb me. I'm a very sound sleeper and shan't stir until my alarm clock rings in the morning.'

Thinking the older woman might like to have the bedroom and bathroom to herself for a while, Nicola said, 'I'll have a glass of wine while you're getting ready for bed and come up in about half an hour.'

In the lounge, slightly to Nicola's irritation, Philip, having sat next to her at dinner, seated himself beside her again. She had hoped to chat to other members of the group.

Never mind, there would be plenty of time to get to know everyone in the next two weeks, she thought, waiting her turn to give an order to the waiter.

The only one she didn't want to know better was Richard Russell. Some contact with him was unavoidable, but she meant to have as little to do with him as possible. Which shouldn't be too difficult as Janet obviously hoped to annex him.

Later, although the bed was comfortable and it had been a long day, she found she couldn't sleep. His presence in the group didn't make for peace of mind.

He revived so many memories she had tried to forget; not only the disruption of her career but also of her personal life. As a side-effect of losing her job, she had lost the man she had been in love with. She was over it now. Her heart was no longer irreparably broken as it had seemed to be for the first eighteen months after the split with Ian.

But the combination of losing her job and her lover had been severe blows to her self-esteem. Meeting Richard again had shown that her *amour propre* wasn't completely healed yet.

Although at first it had angered her that he hadn't the slightest recollection of ever seeing her before, now she realised it was better this way.

The situation would have been much worse if he *had* remembered her.

As he seemed a man who would normally have an excellent memory, she must hope that during the next two weeks of daily contact nothing about her would ring a bell in his mind.

It was bad enough his being part of the group. She could do without the added chagrin of having him suddenly remember that, during the purge he had instigated, she had been one of the first to be jettisoned.

*    *    *

When Nicola and Miss Goodge went in search of breakfast next morning, they expected to be the first comers. Richard Russell was ahead of them.

'Who is your room partner?' Miss Goodge asked him, when they had exchanged good mornings.

'No one. I paid the supplement for a single room to avoid finding myself with a smoker or a snorer.'

'Fortunately neither Nicola nor I fall into either of those categories,' said Miss Goodge.

He smiled. 'Actually the main reason I've arranged to have a room to myself is that I don't need a lot of sleep. Five or six hours is enough. The rest of the time I read, which would be hard lines on anyone sharing a room with me.'

Other members of the group arrived and helped themselves to the bread, white cheese, honey, butter and black and green olives set out on a side table. Coffee and tea were provided in two large urns.

After breakfast they packed their belongings, which were to be left in the hotel's luggage-room to await their return from sightseeing.

Today Janet's outfit seemed more suitable for drinking *Glühwein* or hot chocolate in the cafés of a fashionable ski resort than a day spent walking round Turkish mosques and museums.

At five minutes to ten Nuray arrived to take them to the Blue Mosque by way of the streets surrounding the legendary Grand Bazaar.

'Today being Sunday, it's closed,' she told them. 'But when you come back to Istanbul at the end of the trek you'll have plenty of time for shopping. There are one thousand shops in sixty-seven covered streets. It's easy to lose your way in the bazaar, but it's fun to explore and the shopkeepers are helpful about giving directions.'

At the Blue Mosque they took off their boots and trainers and left them on racks by the door. Nuray took a scarf from her pocket and covered her hair with it.

'This isn't essential but, if you have a scarf with you, it's respectful.'

Inside the huge multi-domed building the floor was spread with dozens, perhaps hundreds of oriental rugs given to the mosque as offerings, the most recent gifts laid over the earlier ones.

Earlier that morning, from a mosque somewhere near the hotel, Nicola had heard the voice of a muezzin calling the faithful to prayer. But at this hour the mosque was almost empty with only a few old men on their knees in the main part of the building, and three or four women praying in the area reserved for females.

Beckoning the group to gather round her, and keeping her voice low, Nuray pointed out various features of special interest, notably the twenty thousand blue Iznik tiles cladding the interior of the building, from which the mosque took its nickname.

'The feminists among you may disapprove of the sexes being segregated,' she said, looking round the group. 'But it would be wrong to assume that women's position in Turkish society is inferior. In the more backward country districts—yes, there are inequalities. But not among educated people. Here in Istanbul there are many women in important positions. Not enough of them yet. But isn't that also true of America and the countries in the European Community?'

When no one made any comment, she said, her dark eyes twinkling, 'My last group had strong feelings on this subject. But perhaps you are more sensible and realise it's better to travel without preconceived ideas and to form your own opinions from what you see and hear in the next two weeks.'

The rest of the morning was spent at another of the city's great landmarks, the church of St Sophia built in the sixth century.

'Ten thousand men worked for six years to make it the most magnificent building in the world,' said Nuray. 'The doors were of ivory, amber and cedar, the columns of white and green marble from Egypt and Syria. While they were making the mosaics on the walls and ceilings—four acres of them—the Byzantines invented the technique of covering a cube with gold leaf and sealing it with molten glass.'

In spite of the ravages wreaked on it during the intervening centuries, the church was still a breathtaking building. But after an hour of admiring its splendours most of the group were glad when Nuray announced it was time for lunch.

She took them to the Pudding Shop, explaining it had once been a famous meeting place for hippies in transit between Europe and India.

In the restaurant they lined up to choose from a selection of hot dishes. All the ground-floor tables being taken, the group ate in the room upstairs, split up at several tables.

Reluctantly, as she would have preferred not to be at his table, Nicola found herself with no choice but to share with Richard, Janet and the much older man called Miles.

The two men chatted knowledgeably about the construction of the church until the arrival of a bottle of wine.

Evidently Richard and Janet had agreed to share a bottle as, before he uncorked it, the waiter gave them each a wine glass.

'Two more glasses, please?' said Richard. 'Our friends might also like to try some Turkish wine.'

His reference to herself and Miles as friends was ironic in the circumstances, thought Nicola. Of course it was only a polite manner of speaking and he had no idea that to one of the people at the table he came close to being an enemy.

'Not for me, thanks,' she said, shaking her head, when the waiter returned with the additional glasses. 'I'm having apple tea.'

'The bread is first-rate,' said Miles, helping himself to a crusty chunk from the basket. 'If the bread we've had so far is typical, there should be no problem with the picnics we'll be having later on. I'm looking forward to that part of the trip. I'm not very keen on cities. You three are all Londoners, I believe?'

'I find big cities exciting,' said Janet. She looked at Richard. 'Don't you?'

'I have to spend a lot of my time in them and I do enjoy certain aspects. But I was born on an island off Cape Cod and I miss the sea when I haven't seen it for a while.'

'How about you, Miss Temple?' Miles asked.

'Nicola,' she corrected, smiling at him. 'I was born in the country. I'm not a true Londoner.'

As she spoke, she caught Richard looking at her more intently than before. Could it be that Miles's use of her surname had rung a faint bell in his memory? Was he wondering why 'Nicola Temple' seemed vaguely familiar? Or perhaps she was only imagining a keener look in those extraordinarily blue eyes.

'But you like it there?' Miles persisted. 'You find the rewards offset the drawbacks, do you?'

'Like most people, I don't have much option. It's where I earn my living.'

'If you're a secretary, your options are wide open,' said Richard. 'Is there anyone who has a better range of job choices than a first-class secretary? I shouldn't think so.'

Wanting to switch the conversation away from herself, Nicola turned to Janet. 'Does your work involve much travel or is it mainly in London?'

'We advise anyone, anywhere, who has management difficulties. Last year I went to Japan to study their management systems. I love travelling, although of course when it's business I don't "rough it" as we're going to on this trip.'

'You sound like a dedicated career-woman,' was Richard's comment.

'I'm deeply involved in my work,' Janet agreed. 'But then I'm sure you are too.'

'What is your field, Richard?' asked Miles. 'I didn't catch everything said at the table last night.'

'I'm a publisher. And you?'

'I'm retired now. I was in the army. What sort of books do you publish?'

'A lot of non-fiction... memoirs, biography, travel. But also literary and middle-brow novels. I'm with Barking & Dollis. You probably have some of our titles on your bookshelves.'

'Indeed I have,' Miles agreed. 'You have some excellent writers. I seldom read novels myself, but my wife used to enjoy them. Unfortunately she was an invalid for the last ten years of her life, dependent on books and the radio to keep her amused. She wasn't keen on television.'

'My favourite entertainments are plays and concerts,' said Janet. 'That's why I could never live in the depths of the country, Miles. I'd miss London's cultural life. Have you seen the new play at the Haymarket, Richard?'

'Not yet.' He looked at Nicola. 'Have you?'

She shook her head. 'I don't often go to the theatre. What's good about London for me is the number of things which are free... art shows, street markets and so on. I'm gradually working my way round all the smaller museums.'

'I'm surprised we haven't run into each other. I'm a museum buff too,' he told her, smiling.

She was aware of his charm, but although it might work on Janet it had no effect on her. She knew too much about him. The virile good looks and polished manners were merely a façade. The inner man was both tough and ruthless; a worthy scion of the American forebears who had amassed a multi-media fortune and, on his mother's side, the long line of Englishmen whose ambition and cunning had brought them titles and estates.

The night train was due to leave Haydarpasa Station at half-past five. Nuray gave them the choice of crossing the Bosporus by coach via the inter-continental bridge, or by ferry.

As the day had grown steadily colder, most people chose the coach. Nicola, snug in her down-filled jacket, wasn't troubled by the falling temperature and was keen to see the city's famous skyline from the deck of the ferry. Going over the Bosporus by a bridge, inside a tour bus, seemed an unadventurous way of crossing the boundary between Europe and Asia.

When Nuray finished counting the hands of those who preferred the coach and said, 'OK, now who's for the ferry?' Nicola put up her hand, unaware that in the seats behind her only one other person had abstained from the previous vote.

The ferry dock was near Galata Bridge, the main link between the old and new parts of the city. Close by were the berths of the fishing-boats with swarthy fishermen tossing bags of fish to customers standing on the quay, and fresh fish being charcoal-grilled and sold between hunks of bread or wrapped in unleavened *pide*.

'I'll see the rest of you later,' said Nuray, when the coach had stopped. 'The driver knows where to take you.'

She climbed down to the roadway followed by Nicola and then, to Nicola's dismay, by Richard—and only Richard.

'Have I time to buy a fish sandwich?' he asked.

'Yes, if you like.'

'Shall I get three?'

Nuray shook her head. 'Not for me, thank you. But Nicola might like one.'

'No, thanks.'

Although the fish couldn't be fresher, Nicola felt it might not be wise to eat bread handled by cooks who had spent all day on the wharf. Warned by her much-travelled brother about things to avoid, she didn't want to risk picking up a bug, especially with a night on a train and the first day of trekking ahead of her.

After Richard had bought his snack, Nuray paid for the metal tokens they needed to get through the turnstile on to the landing stage.

'I'm afraid it's going to be crowded. This is a busy time of day and with Istanbul's population up to ten million our transport systems are stretched to their limits.'

At the end of a wintry afternoon, most of the passengers wanted to be under cover and the two foreigners and their guide had no difficulty in finding places by the rail on the open deck.

'At least try a small piece of fish,' said Richard, opening his sandwich and offering it to Nicola. 'Break a little bit off with your fingers. Fish straight from the heat of the grill isn't likely to carry any germs, if that worries you about street food.'

Taking off her right glove, she detached a piece of hot fish and put it in her mouth.

'It's delicious.' She licked her fingers. 'Thank you.'

Richard sank his teeth into the bread and bit off a mouthful, chewing it with obvious enjoyment. 'Mmm...the best food I've had so far,' he said presently. 'I should have bought two and kept one for later. I doubt if the train's restaurant car will have anything better to offer.'

With a blast of her siren the steamer began to move downstream.

'This waterway isn't the Bosporus. This is the Golden Horn,' said Nuray. 'If you like, when we come back to Istanbul, we can take a boat trip along the Bosporus as far as the Black Sea. Would you excuse me for a moment? I've seen someone I know. I must go and say hello.'

Although they were surrounded by people, the Turkish girl's sudden departure left Nicola sharply conscious of

being alone in the company of the last man in the world
with whom she wished to have a *tête-à-tête*.

'Quite a spectacular view,' he said, looking upstream
at the hillsides crowded with old and new buildings,
domes, minarets and towers.

She murmured agreement, inwardly amazed that she
should be seeing it with him, of all people, beside her.

'That must be Seraglio Point where the sultans had
their discarded concubines drowned,' said Richard, a few
minutes later. 'There were often quite a number of
foreign girls in the harem, I believe. Reluctant recruits
who'd been captured and sold by pirates and brigands.'
There was a slight glint in his eyes as he looked down
at her. 'Had you been travelling without a protector in
those times, you'd have stood a good chance of becoming an unwilling odalisque.'

She said, 'Most women were slaves then anyway. It
probably wasn't much worse being a sultan's concubine
than a European wife with a despotic husband.'

'I don't think the ones who ended up in a weighted
sack at the bottom of the Bosporus would have agreed
with you, poor little wretches.'

'You may feel sorry for them now, but I expect, if
you'd lived in those times and been a sultan or a pasha,
you'd have had a harem like everyone else with the means
and opportunity,' she said crisply.

He looked amused. 'I might—yes. But it wasn't only
the concubines who had a hard time. So did the sultan's
younger brothers. They spent their lives in a place called
the Golden Cage, and their concubines had to have their
ovaries removed. If any did become pregnant, they were
drowned.'

They were both leaning on the rail and suddenly he
moved closer so that their arms were touching. The
contact had no significance. It was forced on him by a
stout man pushing between Richard and the person on
the other side of him in order to spit something into the
water below. Nor, because of their cold-weather clothing,

was it the intimate contact it would have been on a warm day.

'Sorry to crowd you,' said Richard.

His apology made the fat man glance at him. He grinned, showing appalling teeth, and said something to Richard in Turkish, at the same time giving him a friendly clap on the shoulder.

To Nicola's surprise, Richard answered him in what she took to be Turkish.

It didn't seem to surprise the fat man, who responded even more affably and then noticed Nicola. To her surprise and discomfiture he gave her the appraising look she had seen Turkish men giving Sylvie while they were sightseeing.

This was followed by a nudge in Richard's ribs, another remark and a hearty guffaw, releasing a strong gust of garlic fumes. Then with another slap on Richard's back, he left them.

'How come you speak Turkish?' she asked, as Richard moved back to his previous position.

'I don't . . . only a few useful phrases. He was obviously being friendly, so I said the Turkish equivalent of, "Hello, glad to know you; how are you?"' He gave her another of his amused looks. 'I understood what he said about you because it's an old Turkish proverb. "The beauty of a woman is measured in kilos". He mistook the padding in your jacket for the cuddlesome curves Turks in his age-group admire.'

'You must have a very retentive memory.' For some things, she added mentally.

'I had the good luck to be born with what's sometimes called a photographic memory. It doesn't mean I remember everything I see or read. But when I want to retain something, usually I can.'

All Nicola's reasons for disliking him, which had been in temporary abeyance, swiftly revived.

Clearly he hadn't wanted to retain the names and faces of the people he had sacked three years ago, she thought, averting her face.

Just then Nuray came back. 'I'm sorry I deserted you. Are you freezing to death?'

She looked, thought Nicola, very beautiful with her black curls blowing round her face and her olive skin given a rosy hue by the cold.

That Richard was thinking the same thing was evident in his expression as he disclaimed being cold.

'But you're not as warmly wrapped as we are. You should have stayed on the coach, Nuray. This trip is no novelty for you and we could have managed by ourselves. I have a few words of Turkish.'

'You do? That's unusual. Most tourists don't bother even to learn to say thank you.'

Nicola had bothered and had already said *tesekkür* several times, but she didn't say so.

'I expect my accent is atrocious.' Richard said something in Turkish and raised an enquiring eyebrow.

Nuray's dark eyes sparkled with laughter. 'No, your accent is good, but where did you learn to say *that*? Not from a language book, I'm sure.'

'No, from a Turk in London.'

'Ah, that explains it.'

What had he said to her? Nicola wondered. Judging by Nuray's expression, something complimentary and possibly mildly risqué. But clearly she didn't object to him flirting with her. If she had no steady boyfriend it must make her job more enjoyable when a group of trekkers included an attractive unattached man.

The ferry was approaching its berth on the far side of the straits. Very soon they would disembark in Asia.

# CHAPTER THREE

BEFORE they boarded the train, Nuray held a briefing on the platform.

'There are two compartments reserved for us. The allocation of bunks is based on my experience of these journeys. It's better for the top bunks to be occupied by the most agile members of the group. As we shall be leaving the train at four-thirty in the morning, and most people sleep partly dressed, I'm sure you won't mind sharing your compartment with members of the opposite sex.'

After a pause to see if anyone disagreed, she went on, 'Here is the plan I have worked out. If you don't like my arrangements, please tell me. I don't want anyone to be unhappy.'

She held up a clipboard with two groups of names written as large as the sheet of paper would permit.

Scanning the list, Nicola saw that she had been given a middle bunk opposite Janet. Philip would be sleeping above her with Richard in the other top bunk. The bottom bunks were allocated to the married couple, Bob and Joan Tufnell.

'You'll find there's a place for your kitbags alongside the top bunks, above the train's corridor,' said Nuray. 'When the luggage has been stowed, there'll be time to buy drinks and snacks from the station kiosks before we leave at five-thirty. Please make sure you're on board at five twenty-five. We don't want anyone left behind.'

For twelve people, all with a large kitbag and most with a day-pack as well, to make their way along a narrow corridor and arrange themselves and their baggage in the confined space of two railway carriages could have resulted in a confused scrimmage and possibly some frayed tempers.

But whatever happened next door, in Nicola's compartment Richard took charge of the operation. If his self-appointed command was resented by the two other men, neither objected to being told what to do, or to the authoritative tone of a man who might give his orders in the form of suggestions but nevertheless expected to have them obeyed without argument.

Nuray appeared in the doorway. 'If you want to do some shopping, I'll keep an eye on your things. Later, when we all go to the restaurant, the conductor will lock the compartments for us.'

At one of the station kiosks, Nicola bought a bottle of water, chocolate and a ring-shaped bread roll called a *simit* scattered with sesame seeds.

She had never travelled by a night train before and found the bustle of the station, the babble of Turkish voices and the fact that she was now in Asia, *en route* to the Taurus Mountains, very exciting.

To her brother Peter this kind of adventure was commonplace. But her own foreign holidays had been limited to a school trip to Italy, a week in Spain with her ex-boyfriend and a few days in the Dordogne region of France, working on a manuscript with an author who lived there.

Remembering that book and her enthusiasm for it, she sighed as she walked back to the train.

Richard had returned to the carriage before her and was there on his own, peeling a lemon.

'Can I interest you in a gin and tonic? No ice, I'm afraid, and I'm using slices of lemon rather than twists of peel.'

Tempted by the offer, yet reluctant to be beholden to him in any way, Nicola decided that for this one night, in these special circumstances, she would try to forget they had met before and pretend he was just another trekker.

'Yes, please.'

He had just poured a generous slosh of gin into her plastic mug when Janet and Philip came back.

'Happy hour!' said Richard. 'The drinks are on me but you'll have to supply the containers.'

The train was late starting. When at last it did move, it didn't pick up much speed. Sipping a second round of drinks and eating Turkish crisps provided by Bob and Joan, they passed seemingly endless blocks of suburban apartments.

By now it had begun to snow and the daylight was fading rapidly. The temperature inside the train was starting to rise.

Nuray appeared in the corridor and slid back the door of their carriage. 'We've been discussing what time to have dinner. The restaurant isn't large. To be sure of sitting together, we should go early.'

'The sooner we eat, the sooner we can turn in,' said Bob. 'It's going to be a short night.'

Most of the tables in the restaurant car were for four people, with tables for two on the other side of the aisle. As yet there was no one there but the two check-waist-coated waiters and a man drinking tea.

Nicola sat with Miles and two people with whom neither she nor anyone else had so far had much to do. She knew their names were Stuart Ladbroke and Lorna Wood but up to now they had been engrossed in each other. Tonight they seemed more sociable and very soon Miles and Stuart discovered a mutual interest in birdlife.

This subject appeared to bore Lorna. 'I'm not crazy about ancient cities either,' she confided to Nicola. 'But Stuart had booked this holiday before we met and he didn't want to change it so I said I'd come. Last winter I went to the Seychelles. The boyfriend I had then was crazy about snorkelling. I just lay on the beach all day and in the evening we went dancing. It was great.'

But it wasn't diplomatic to mention it while her current boyfriend was monitoring their conversation with one ear, thought Nicola.

While the other girl continued to talk about the bargain-price leather coats and bags she had heard were to be found in Turkey, Nicola's thoughts turned back four years to her own experience of holidaying with a man.

That too had been a walking tour, but not with a group. She and Ian had been on their own, staying in a small Spanish *hostal* and spending their days exploring the surrounding countryside. At that time of year, late February, the almond groves had been in blossom.

Her parents had liked Ian and, although they hadn't really approved of her going on holiday with him, they had accepted that times had changed since their day and it might not be a bad thing for young people to be on the closest possible terms before committing themselves to marriage.

Oddly enough it had been her brother Peter who had disapproved of the holiday. He had never liked Ian and subsequent events had proved him right. When she had lost her job, Ian, who was also in publishing, had seemed to feel her dismissal would be prejudicial to his prospects. He hadn't actually dropped her like a hot potato, but he hadn't wanted to be seen with her at publishing functions and the time they spent together had dwindled. Eventually she had heard he was seeing someone else. When asked if it was true, he had admitted that it was. It had been the end of her first and only love-affair.

A burst of laughter from the next table brought her back to the present. Looking past Lorna, still in full spate about clothes, Nicola gathered that Richard had just told an amusing anecdote. He wasn't laughing himself, but his expression was amused and the others at his table were falling about.

Perhaps, in a way, she should be grateful to him. He had ruined her career but had saved her from a future disaster in her private life. If he hadn't sacked her, Ian might have married her, only to let her down later.

Presently, at Richard's suggestion, the women returned to the carriage to prepare for bed ahead of the men. He and Philip had lowered the six couchettes before the compartment was locked.

Janet was the first to try out the train's facilities.

'The washrooms aren't good, but the WCs are unspeakable!' she reported, with an exaggerated shudder.

'Never mind,' Joan said comfortably. 'It's only for this one night, and we knew it wouldn't be the Orient Express, didn't we? The brochure warned us to be prepared for primitive conditions at times.'

Nicola's brother had also briefed her on what he jokingly called the Turkish Loo Experience. She returned from her trip along the corridor still smiling at the thought of how various people she knew would react to it.

Joan had gone to one of the washrooms and Janet was standing in the aisle between the bunks, creaming her hands.

'You found it amusing?' she said, raising her eyebrows.

Nicola nodded. 'If you imagine the most pompous person you know crouching over a hole in the floor in a moving train, with no hand-holds, it does conjure some rather hilarious visions, don't you think?'

'No, I do not!' said Janet emphatically. 'I shall travel first class on the way back—if this ghastly train has a first class.'

'Why did you come on this holiday if you don't like roughing it?'

'If you want to meet interesting men it's no use going on a cruise or to one of the luxury resorts,' said Janet, with unexpected candour. 'Cruises are seething with widows. Luxury resorts are full of married men, elderly lechers and on-the-make toyboys. It's an unfortunate fact of life that attractive men are mainly found doing uncomfortable things like trekking, sailing and pot-holing.

I do draw the line at that, but some degree of discomfort seems inevitable.'

'Doesn't your work bring you into contact with lots of men?' Nicola asked.

'Mostly they're married. Who needs that kind of hassle? Both Richard and Philip are single. Philip's not my type, but Richard is.'

'If you're staking a claim, don't worry,' Nicola told her drily. 'Neither of them is my type.'

They were in their bunks, with the curtains drawn across the corridor windows, when a tap on the glass announced the return of the men.

Nicola was reading by the dim light from the ceiling. The couchettes had neither curtains nor individual reading lamps.

'Feel free to use my bunk as a step to get up to yours,' Janet said to Richard.

'Thanks, but that won't necessary. Bob's berth is the one we'll use.' He reached for his day-pack, took out a wet pack and disappeared again.

Philip was the first to return from his ablutions. Watching his awkward clamber into the bunk above hers made Nicola wonder why he had chosen this holiday. Although slim, he was far from agile. Maybe his reason was the reverse of Janet's: he hoped to meet the single women he didn't encounter at work or in his normal social life.

When Richard returned to the carriage, he unlaced his heavy boots, placed them neatly together by the door, stepped lightly on the edge of Bob's bunk and with a single lithe movement swung himself up to the bunk above Janet's.

There, with economical movements suggesting that it wasn't the first time he had undressed in a confined space, he shed both his shirt and trousers and folded them.

Nicola hadn't meant to watch him undress but she had been distracted from her book by the muscular movement which had taken him from the floor to the upper berth. Now, revealed by the close-fitting T-shirt he was wearing under his outer shirt, his upper arms showed powerful muscles between shoulder and elbow.

To her chagrin, he caught her looking at him. 'If you want to go on reading, I have a good flashlight you can borrow.'

'I have a torch, thanks. But I'm going to try to sleep. Goodnight.'

She closed her book, turned towards the wall and lay down.

'Is everyone ready for lights out?' he asked.

Everyone was, and after a chorus of goodnights and rustling movements there was silence in the compartment apart from the rumbling of the train's wheels and the comings and goings in the corridor.

Nicola slept fitfully, waking each time the train stopped. Sometimes she dozed but mostly she lay thinking about Janet's reason for coming on this trip and her own non-existent love-life.

She had set the alarm on her watch to go off half an hour before they were due to disembark. But what roused her from a doze was the overhead light being switched on, followed by an irritable exclamation from the bunk above her.

'Sorry, but it's time we were up,' said Richard. Already dressed, he returned his own bunk to its upright position.

This allowed the unflatteringly hard light of the fluorescent tubes to fall full on Janet. She was wearing a black silk eye-mask. Like Nicola, she had slept in silk thermals, but Nicola's top had a round neckline and she was wearing a light sports bra under it. Janet's had a low V-neck which, as she pushed up the mask and raised herself on her elbows, gave an arresting view of her unsupported breasts, their shape clearly outlined by the fine silk jersey fabric.

As he finished securing his bunk, Richard could hardly have failed to notice them, thought Nicola.

Not that his activities had been arrested by the display of Janet's opulent curves. He said, 'Show a leg, Philip. Once you're out, we can close your bunk and give Nicola some headroom.'

Muttering complaints at being disturbed, Philip landed on the floor with a heavy thud. When his bunk had been stowed and Richard had left the compartment, he said to Nicola, 'What a bloody awful time of night to be dragged out of bed. I haven't slept much, have you?'

'Enough,' she said cheerfully, slipping her feet into her boots. 'Give me a shove with my bunk, will you? Then Bob will have some headroom.'

Nuray appeared. 'When the train stops, please don't dawdle. We must get off as quickly as possible,' she warned them. 'If you look outside, you'll see there's been heavy snow in this area, so you'll need your warmest clothes. It will be cold crossing the mountains.'

With six people trying to dress and pack their belongings in a confined space, they would never have been ready if Richard hadn't organised them, especially as both Janet and Philip admitted to being useless without the cup of strong coffee they both needed to get them going.

'Coffee comes later. Right now you have to hustle or you'll be trekking solo from somewhere down the line, and that could be awkward,' Richard said, folding Janet's bedding for her.

With his help she was ready when the train began to slow down.

'Can't see any sign of a station,' said Bob, peering out of the window.

Nicola was already in the corridor with her kitbag. The conductor beckoned her to follow him. By the time

they reached the door at the end of the corridor, the
train was almost at a standstill.

Outside there was nothing to be seen but the thick
snow lying on the ground in the area illuminated by the
lights of the train. Beyond that there was only darkness.

The train stopped. The conductor climbed down and,
turning, reached up for her kitbag. As she handed it to
him with a grateful, '*Tesekkür*,' there was a shout from
near by and someone came running up.

She was confronted by a man with a thick crop of
curly black hair, snapping black eyes and a wide grin.

'Good morning...welcome. I'm Serif, your driver.
Let me help you.'

As if she were a young child, he put his hands under
her armpits and with no visible effort swung her off her
feet and set her on the frozen grass.

'This,' said Miss Goodge, a few minutes later, 'is how
I imagine Siberia. Where exactly are we, I wonder?'

As she spoke, her warm breath turned to puffs of
vapour in the icy night air.

No one answered her question. Nuray and the new-
comer were deep in conversation and the others were
still adjusting to the sub-zero temperature.

Thankful for the loan of her brother's jacket and two
pairs of socks inside her boots, Nicola watched the train
starting to move and waved to the conductor as he continued his journey, leaving his two compatriots and the
group of foreigners standing beside the track.

'Come along.' Serif led the way to a large four-wheel-
drive truck of the type used for transport in deserts and
other difficult terrain.

Leaping aboard and helping the women to hoist their
baggage up the steep steps, he showed them how to open
the baggage lockers under the two long rows of sideways-
facing seats.

'As there aren't many of you, there's plenty of room to make yourselves comfortable. Soon we'll stop for a hot drink.'

Leaving them to decide where to sit, he sprang down the steps and went to the separate driver's cab. Moments later there was a hiss like an air brake and the double doors at the nearside rear of the truck slid into their closed position. The engine roared. The truck jolted and bounced over some yards of rough ground before turning on to a roadway. From the cab came a cheery triple blast on the horn as Serif accelerated, making it clear why the two rows of seats had sturdy metal foot-rails fitted to the floor in front of them.

The roadside café, heated by a closed stove, where they were served with glasses of sweet tea, was the Turkish equivalent of a lorry drivers' pull-in.

'Now everyone feels better—yes?' Serif asked, when the glasses were being refilled by a man who, like him, hadn't shaved since yesterday morning.

Their dark stubble made Nicola notice that the only man present with a smooth jaw was Richard. He must have shaved last thing last night.

Mrs Tufnell joined them, a cheerful-faced busty woman in her fifties, with permed brown hair turning grey.

'You're not superstitious, I hope,' she greeted them. 'With the driver, we're thirteen.'

'As far as I'm concerned, the important thing about Serif is whether he's a safe driver. He's certainly fast,' Nicola said drily.

He was standing by the stove, one hand tucked in the pocket of his black leather windcheater, the other holding a glass of tea. He caught her eye and came over.

'You know my name, but I don't know yours.'

She introduced the two older women, after which Miss Goodge asked them all to call her Hilary.

'Hilary...Joan...and Nicola,' he repeated. 'Is this your first time in Turkey?'

They told him it was and Hilary asked, 'How far are we driving today?'

'A long way. But you can sleep and later we'll stop for breakfast. I'm the only one who must stay awake,' he said, smiling. 'Don't worry. I'm not tired. I went to bed early last night.'

'You speak very good English,' said Joan.

'Of course. You don't speak Turkish, do you? So I must speak English...and German. We have many German tourists.'

When Richard joined them, Hilary said, 'With you two big chaps in the party, we should survive whatever amazing adventures the trip has in store for us. Richard, this is Serif. Serif...Richard.'

The men shook hands and smiled at each other, but it seemed to Nicola that there was a certain wariness in the looks they exchanged.

Before they could have any conversation, Serif was called away by the café's proprietor.

'He seems nice,' said Joan. 'We've struck lucky with the people in charge of us, haven't we? Bob and I've been on holidays where we hardly ever saw the couriers and they weren't all that friendly when they did condescend to appear.'

'Really? Perhaps you've been unlucky,' said Hilary. 'All the couriers and guides I've encountered have been very good at their jobs. What's your experience, Richard?'

'It's the first guided tour I've been on. I didn't choose this trip. It was booked by a friend who's interested in classical archaeology. A few days ago his father was taken seriously ill and is probably going to die. Sam couldn't leave his mother to cope on her own. He was going to cancel the holiday but I said I'd come in his place.'

'So you're here on impulse,' said Hilary.

'That's right. I needed a break, the tickets were there for the taking and here I am. Whether I'll regret it remains to be seen. We do seem to have struck an exceptionally cold spell. But maybe the weather will be better once we're over the mountains. May I get you some more tea, ladies?'

'He's very nice too,' said Joan approvingly, as he took her glass to be refilled. She gave Nicola a roguish glance. 'With him and Philip and now a good-looking driver, there's plenty of talent, as our daughter would say. It's no fun for you younger people if a group's all one sex, is it?'

'To me Serif looks as if he may be a bit of a brigand where girls are concerned,' said Hilary. 'I'd expect him to target Sylvie as being the most impressionable. She's gazing at him now.'

So was Lorna, Nicola noticed. While Stuart was talking to Philip, Lorna was eyeing Serif.

The long drive south was less of an ordeal for Nicola than for some of the others.

She had with her a sheepskin foot-muff, borrowed from her mother, and with this, and her sleeping-bag tucked round her legs, she scarcely felt the cold numbing the feet of others less well-equipped.

What none of them realised until after the tea-stop was that the truck's heater had broken down. It was warm in the driver's cab. They could see through the window at the back of it that Serif had shed his black jacket and Nuray her thick dark overcoat. But the back of the truck was like a refrigerator, and, while the two couples on board could huddle together for warmth, those on their own had only their clothes and other wrappings to protect them from the Arctic conditions.

Although the interior lights were on, they were too dim and the truck was jolting too much to make reading possible. How anyone could sleep was a mystery to

Nicola, but several people seemed to be dozing, including the two on either side of Richard.

After a while she put on her head-set and passed the time listening to music. By the time she had played both sides of the cassette the sky was starting to lighten, gradually revealing long vistas of rolling hills.

On the other side of the truck Sylvie, deep asleep, was lolling against Richard. He didn't seem to mind. Although his eyes were scanning the view through the windows in Nicola's side, she had the impression that his thoughts were elsewhere.

Full daylight brought no relief from the cold. The journey began to seem interminable. By flexing her toes and ankles inside the fleecy muff, Nicola kept the blood coursing through them. But for some of the others cold feet were becoming painful.

At last they came to a small town. To everyone's relief the truck stopped outside a café. It wasn't the sort of establishment any of them would have chosen for a coffee-stop in Europe. But this was rural Asia Minor.

'Ooh, let me get close to that stove!' Joan exclaimed, making a bee-line for the source of the café's warmth. 'My poor feet feel like lumps of ice.'

'On the other side of the mountains it will be warm,' Serif promised. 'Maybe not tomorrow, but the next day you will be swimming.'

A chorus of sceptical comments greeted this statement.

'It's true, I promise you. Look——' He unbuttoned his shirt to display a deeply tanned chest. 'This is from lying in the sun on the beach where you'll be swimming. If you don't believe me, ask Nuray.'

'The weather is usually very nice,' the Turkish girl confirmed. 'We've come a long way from Istanbul and we still have some way to go. The sun will be shining when we get to Antalya.'

'Why is the heater kaput? asked Richard. 'Can't it be repaired?'

'Serif will have it mended. I'm sorry it's cold for you. There's room for one more person in the front if anyone would like to join us.'

'I'm staying with Bob,' said Joan.

'I brought a hot-water bottle,' said Hilary. 'Would you ask them to refill it for me, Nuray?'

The Turkish girl smiled and nodded. 'Would you like to come in the front with us, Janet?' she enquired.

Richard came over to Nicola. 'What were you listening to with that rapt expression on your face?' he asked.

'It could have been one of several things. The tape is a recording made for me by my brother. It's a mixture of favourite pieces to save me bringing a lot of tapes.'

'Is your brother in the music business?'

She shook her head. 'He's an expert on travelling light.'

'If you run out of books, I have two or three you might like. Which guide book did you bring?'

'The one recommended in the Amazing Adventures travel pack.'

He said, 'I've read it. It's not as good as the one published by my people. We have an excellent travel list.'

The remark revived her antagonism. She was tempted to flash back, I had a good list too—until you scrapped it.

Common sense kept her silent. This wasn't the time or the place for a confrontation.

She restricted herself to saying, with a marked lack of interest, 'Really?' before turning to speak to someone else.

Perhaps even that was unwise. He could hardly fail to recognise the brush-off and be annoyed by it. Men like Richard Russell weren't accustomed to receiving signals that their conversation wasn't interesting.

# CHAPTER FOUR

DURING breakfast, a long-distance coach drew up outside. Most of the disembarking women passengers wore headscarves arranged to cover their foreheads and fall on their shoulders. One old lady wore baggy Turkish trousers but the girl on whose arm she was leaning, perhaps her granddaughter, was dressed in jeans and a fashionable sweater.

'*Their* bus is heated,' Lorna said, pouting.

Overhearing her, Serif gave her his dazzling black-eyed smile. 'But now you've had a good breakfast and when you see our beautiful mountains you won't care about a little cold. Why not come beside me in the cab?'

'She's with me,' Stuart said curtly.

'Ah...I see.' Serif inclined his head in amused acknowledgment of the fact that Lorna was private property.

Later, as they left the restaurant, he said to Nicola, 'The man sitting next to you...is he your boyfriend?'

'I met Philip in Istanbul the day before yesterday.'

'And the girl sleeping with her head on the big guy's shoulder? Is she with him?' Clearly he had been watching the trekkers through his inside rear-view mirror.

She shook her head. 'Apart from Joan and her husband, and Stuart and Lorna, all the rest of us are singles.'

'That's good.'

'Why?'

'Because that's the reason for holidays. To make new friends...perhaps to fall in love...like Nuray's sister and her English husband. Perhaps you'll find a Turkish boyfriend. You're a lovely girl...the kind Turkish men like.'

50

Nicola laughed. 'I may have a boyfriend at home.'

'But no one important. If he existed, he wouldn't let you come here without him.'

'Everyone on board, please,' called Nuray.

There were others who hadn't yet boarded, but Nicola had the feeling the summons was directed at her. Maybe Nuray didn't like Serif flirting with the female trekkers, either because they might take him too seriously or because the Turkish girl had her own eye on him.

As the highway ascended the pass over the Taurus Mountains, it became even colder. The scenery was magnificent with snow-covered peaks and crags towering on every side, but soon the view was obscured by ice forming on the windows.

Hanging on to the overhead hand-rail, Hilary came from her place at the rear and said to Nicola, 'If you and I share your quilt, Philip can borrow my rug.'

Miles was dozing, his chin on his chest. Taking care not to disturb him, Nicola sat down in the empty seat next to his and spread her unzipped sleeping-bag across Hilary's legs and her own.

'It was foolish of Philip not to provide himself with all the necessaries,' said Hilary, the noise of the engine and the Turkish music being relayed from Serif's radio ensuring that this remark wouldn't reach his ears. 'We had clear instructions on what to bring. I suppose he didn't bother to read them. It wouldn't surprise me to find that he hasn't brought any books either. What did you bring?'

Sylvie had fallen asleep again but not, this time, with her coppery head on Richard's shoulder. Cocooned in her striped sleeping-bag, she was lying curled up across two seats.

From Sylvie, Nicola's gaze shifted to the strongly marked profile of the man she had snubbed. She regretted it now, knowing it had sprung from pique, because he had no recollection of seeing her before. And he wouldn't let it pass, she felt sure. Somehow, sooner or later, he would make that snub boomerang.

Absently studying his profile while listening to Hilary talking about Turkish literature, Nicola saw that everything she had been told about Richard Russell was there in his strongly marked profile, his intelligence indicated by the high forehead from which his dark hair sprang as thickly but without the curling disorder of Serif's hair.

Her gaze moved downwards past the bridge of his nose to the aggressive thrust of his chin. Between those two bony projections were the softer lines of his mouth, the amorous curve of the lower lip endorsing the rumours about his penchant for beautiful, stylish women.

According to the publishing grapevine, mere glamour wasn't enough. It was said that his girlfriends had to be as diverting conversationally as they were between the sheets.

A tall order, thought Nicola. I wonder if they get as good as they give?

The road was descending now. Soon the ice on the windows had turned to moisture which Richard wiped away with a cloth he found in a locker at the front of the truck.

For the next hour the way was downhill. Occasionally they passed ramshackle, isolated dwellings or small clusters of houses, but there was no sign of a café on this stretch of highway.

People were starting to grumble when suddenly the truck stopped, the rear door wheezed open and Nuray appeared.

'As it's on our way to Antalya we are going to visit the ruins of Termessos,' she told them. 'It's an easy walk which you'll like after sitting for so long.'

'I'm *starving*!' Sylvie exclaimed, emerging from her bag, her cheeks flushed from her long nap.

'You didn't eat enough breakfast,' Richard reminded her.

'I don't like cheese first thing in the morning.'

'It's what the Turks like for breakfast, so either you eat it or go hungry,' he said unsympathetically.

To Nicola's disappointment, their accommodation at Antalya wasn't a timber-built *pansiyon* in the old part of the city, but a small modern hotel off one of the main shopping streets.

Nor was she to share with Hilary as she had expected.

'For the first week of the trek we find it best for the single people to have different room-mates each time we move to a new place,' Nuray explained, before handing out their keys. 'In this way everyone makes friends more quickly—especially the shy people.'

She referred to her clipboard. 'Tonight Hilary is sharing with Sylvie, and Janet with Nicola.'

'I shouldn't think this place has been built long. Everything looks brand-new,' said Janet, flopping wearily on to one of the twin beds in their room. 'I'm bushed! Being woken in the middle of the night doesn't suit my metabolism. You can have the shower first.'

When, swathed in a large white bath-towel, her wet head wrapped in a smaller one, Nicola returned to the bedroom, Janet was asleep.

Nicola left her undisturbed while she rough-dried and combed her hair. Then, because she wanted to use her dryer and there wasn't time for Janet to have a long nap, she gave her a gentle shake.

Janet was still doing her face when Nicola went down to the lobby and walked outside to enjoy the sun on her face. Richard was there before her.

In view of her offhand response to his remark at the breakfast stop, she wondered if he would ignore her. But it seemed his punctilious manners were too deeply ingrained to allow him to be discourteous, whatever he might feel inwardly.

Rising from the low stone wall where he had been sitting, he said pleasantly, 'A hot shower is a great reviver, isn't it?'

'It was wonderful.' Impulsively, she added, 'I was rather abrupt at the café this morning. Put it down to tiredness, will you?'

For a moment or two he was silent, looking down at her with an expression she couldn't interpret. Then he said, 'No need to apologise. It was understandable.'

What did that mean? That he *did* know who she was and therefore wasn't surprised when her hostility had shown through?

'We were all a bit uptight at breakfast,' he went on. 'Being dumped off a train in the small hours and bounced up and down in that rattle-trap——' with a gesture at the nearby truck '——is enough to jangle anyone's nerves. Here come some of the others.'

They had lunch at a *pide salonu* serving Turkish pizzas.

'If you thought pizza was an Italian idea, you were wrong,' said Nuray. 'It was a Turkish invention. We also gave the world tulips, cherries, parchment and angora wool...and smallpox inoculations were being given in Turkey seventy years before your Dr Jenner introduced vaccination in England. So I think we've made a good contribution to civilisation, don't you?' she asked, smiling.

The restaurant's tables being round ones, the group couldn't sit together. Nicola shared with Stuart, Lorna and Serif, who helped them to choose from the menu.

Nuray came to their table. 'Serif, will you find out what everyone wants to drink, please?'

He nodded. 'What would you like, Nicola? There's no alcohol served here.'

'Water for me, please.'

While he was away from the table and the other two were gazing at a children's programme on the large colour TV, Nicola found herself watching Richard and wondering why she had felt constrained to apologise to him.

The reason wasn't only that it seemed a tactical error to distance herself from anyone with whom she had to live at close quarters for two weeks. It was more complex.

Could it be that, in spite of what he had done to her, she was attracted to him?

When Serif returned, she asked, 'How long have you worked for the tour company?'

'Since I was a student. Our universities have only two terms: from October to January and March to June. In the vacations many students work in the tourist industry. Turkey is a young country. More than half our population is under twenty years old. We have forty universities, but every year there are seven hundred thousand applications for places. I was lucky to get a place. But of course I am very intelligent,' he added, with a grin.

'What subjects were you studying?'

'Languages ... German, French and Italian. Then the company offered me a permanent job as a driver. I know something about motors, you see. I was always interested in them and I can do running repairs if the truck breaks down.'

Nicola wondered if he had actually graduated. If he had, surely he could have got a better job than driving for a tour company? Perhaps he had failed his exams. Or even been sent down for breaking university rules.

Serif said, 'One day I shall be a famous poet.'

'A poet?' she exclaimed, startled. He seemed to have none of the attributes she associated with poets. Everything about him suggested a man of action, not an intellectual, and certainly not one who expressed his ideas in verse.

'Do you like poetry? If you're interested, I'll introduce you to some of our Turkish poets.'

Because poetry seemed an unlikely avocation for him, Nicola couldn't help wondering if this was a tactic he used to charm susceptible-looking female trekkers.

Their food arrived, for Nicola a salad and a generous circle of *pide* topped with melted cheese. The cold in the mountains and the walk to Termessos had made her very hungry and she ate it with relish. Lorna, who had chosen a meat topping, picked at hers with less enthusiasm.

When Serif tried to get a four-way conversation going, she and Stuart responded in monosyllables, apparently more interested in what was happening on the screen.

Eventually, looking at Nicola, Serif raised both eyebrows, shrugged and gave up the effort to draw a livelier response from them.

Later, when Nuray was leading a walk through town, he fell into step beside Nicola. 'The two who sat with us at lunch. Why do they come to Turkey if they only want to watch television?'

Nicola had been pondering that question herself. 'They may have had a row. They're not walking together and at lunch Stuart looked rather tight-lipped.'

'Tight-lipped? I don't know this expression.'

'It means repressing annoyance.'

'My English will improve, talking to you. You have a good vocabulary.'

His eyes were focused on her mouth. Although she felt sure it was part of his technique, she couldn't deny that it sent a faint tremor through her. He was dangerously attractive, this big black-eyed Turk. And clearly adept at seduction. It was just as well he hadn't targeted Sylvie. She wouldn't stand a chance of resisting him.

That night they dined at another small restaurant where a table for thirteen was ready for them.

Earlier Nicola had washed her cotton shirt, rolled it in a towel for half an hour and then left it suspended on a hanger in front of the hot-air unit. Apart from changing her shirt and underclothes, she was wearing the jeans and sweatshirt in which she had started the journey.

But Janet had put on clinging black stretch-velvet leggings, a loose black and silver sweater and oversize large silver hoop earrings. She had also stepped up her make-up.

Nicola sat between Miles and Stuart. Janet was sitting beside Richard, talking with great animation, the earrings catching the light with each shift of her head.

While they ate, a musician played an electronic keyboard. All the other diners were men, Nicola noticed.

The meal concluded with fresh fruit, and Serif had a glass of *raki* with his coffee. The colourless spirit clouded when he topped up the glass with water.

'We call it lion's milk. Try it.' He offered the glass to Sylvie.

She took a small sip, immediately pulling a face and saying, 'Yuck...it's horrible!'

Later, outside the restaurant, Nuray asked what they would like to do for the rest of the evening. The four older people wanted an early night. Nicola decided to join them.

Sylvie asked if the town had discos. Richard said he wanted a brisk walk and would find his own way back to the hotel. His long-legged stride had already taken him a hundred yards in the opposite direction when the five early-nighters left the others discussing the options.

'What it is to be young,' Joan said, a shade wistfully.

Bob tucked his wife's arm through his. 'Being young's not that wonderful, love. We'll have a nice drink of hot chocolate and read in bed for a bit. I reckon we'll enjoy that more than anything they'll be doing and we'll be brighter in the morning. Let's hope they come in quietly and don't disturb us.'

'I haven't the least doubt Sylvie will succeed in disturbing me,' said Hilary. 'Especially if Serif persuades her to overcome her initial aversion to *raki*.'

'Get her tight, do you mean?' said Joan. 'Oh, I don't think that's in his mind. If you ask me, Nicola is the one he fancies. He looked ever so disappointed when you said you were coming back with us, Nicola. So did Janet when Richard went off on his own.'

Nicola laughed. 'I should think Serif's only interest in any of us is guessing the size of our tips at the end of the trip. He probably has a girlfriend in Istanbul.'

'Nicola's got a head on her shoulders,' Bob said approvingly. 'It's Lorna who might take a fancy to Serif, if only to make Stuart jealous. I reckon they've got problems, those two.'

'Who hasn't?' Miles said unexpectedly. 'Problems are part and parcel of the human condition.'

They were on the wide pavement of an esplanade with room to walk five abreast. He was at the outer edge, his tall figure casting the longest shadow as they passed a street lamp.

Glancing sideways at him, it struck Nicola that he and Richard had certain similarities; that this was how Richard would look in thirty years' time.

Tall, spare, active, authoritative.

She wondered if Hilary found Miles attractive. And why, when she was better-looking than Joan, and more intelligent, she had never married.

When I'm Hilary's age, shall I still be on my own? she wondered, with an inward shiver which had nothing to do with the coldness of the night.


'Good morning.'

Alone in the breakfast-room and intent on the fashion show on the ubiquitous television, Nicola hadn't noticed Richard's entrance.

'Good morning.'

Watching him use the coffee urn, she wondered if he would sit with her or at one of the other tables.

'May I join you?'

'Please do,' she said politely.

'I'm surprised we're the only ones down. I'd have thought the muezzin would have woken the dead.'

'One would think so,' she agreed. 'But Janet was still fast asleep when I slipped out for a walk. Did you hear the others come in, or were you out late yourself?'

'I was in bed by ten-thirty. Whatever Antalya's night-life is like in high season, I don't think there's much on offer at this time of year. Not that nightclubs and discos appeal to me. Do you like them?'

She shook her head. 'I enjoy dancing at private parties, but not to mega-decibel pop in crowded clubs. Not even when I was eighteen.'

He looked sideways at her. 'How long ago was that?'

'Eight years.'

'You don't look twenty-six.'

'How old are you?'

'Thirty-four... going on forty-five,' he added wryly.

'Why do you say that?'

'The past few years have been a difficult time. A lot of publishing houses have gone to the wall. Now the power in the book industry is in the hands of the big chains of retail outlets. The firm I work for has kept afloat and solvent, but it's been tough going.'

She wondered why he spoke of the firm he worked for, rather than the firm he ran. Did he really see himself as a cog—even if a super-cog—in the UK wheel of the American mega-corporation founded by his grandfather?

Or could it be that, because he was among people who didn't operate at his level, he was deliberately playing down the power he wielded?

'But haven't you found it rewarding to keep your firm in the black when others were sliding into the red?' she asked.

'In many ways—yes. But there's a down-side. Some years ago a book came out in the States called *When Bad Things Happen to Good People*. That's the side of my work I don't like...making decisions which are going to be bad for good people in order to keep the train on the rails, as they say.'

As he spoke, he was spreading white cheese on a chunk of crusty loaf. Nicola shot a covert look at him. Did he really have no idea that sitting beside him was someone for whom one of his decisions had been catastrophic?

'Part of my problem may be that I never took the time off between school and college, or between college and my first job, that most of my contemporaries did,' he went on. 'I never back-packed around Europe or South-East Asia or wherever. Did you do that?'

'No, I went straight from school to secretarial school and then did some temping until I got my first proper job.'

'You said you worked in a bookshop. Which one?'

'Chatham's.'

She had had the job for eighteen months, having got it on the strength of her computer skills and a glowing reference from her previous employer. Chatham's was arguably the most famous bookshop in the West End of London.

'In a manner of speaking, we're in the same line of business,' said Richard.

'Don't you want to forget about business while you're on holiday?'

'Certain aspects of it, yes. But books are my pleasure as well as my work. I'm not short of other interests. But they're relaxations which have to be fitted in to a pretty tight working schedule. For instance I have a pilot's licence but most of my flying is across the Atlantic with all the other guys with briefcases and the *Financial Times* under their arms. Did you see a movie called *Out of Africa* with Redford and Streep in the main roles?'

'You mean those wonderful shots of the Rift Valley from the air?'

He nodded. 'You liked that sequence too, hmm?'

'It was brilliant...I really felt I was up there in the air with them. It was a great film...I came out of the cinema with red eyes and my bag full of damp tissues,' she admitted.

'Yes, those scenes at the funeral were moving. I had a lump in my throat.'

It surprised her that he should confess to being moved. Often men felt they must hide their deepest emotions.

Her ex-boyfriend had equated masculinity with a permanently stiff upper lip.

Yet no one could look more macho than the man beside her, his tall lithe frame set off by his serviceable walking clothes. But he wasn't ashamed to admit that the touching scene in which Meryl Streep, playing Karen Blixen, had spoken the valediction at her lover's graveside had stirred the same feelings in him as in Nicola, even if not to the extent of making him weep.

Then the moment of unexpected rapport came to an end as they were joined by Hilary.

After saying good morning, she said, 'My current room-mate has to be the most disorganised person I've ever encountered. Her side of our room looks as if a tornado has struck it. Such untidiness drives me mad. I'm sure you wouldn't like it either, Nicola. And how Janet put up with it on our first night in Istanbul is a mystery to me.'

'Perhaps it was she who suggested to Nuray that you should change partners,' said Miles, arriving in time to overhear this remark. 'Thereby spreading the burden, so to speak.'

'You may be right. But as far as I'm concerned one night with Sylvie is enough. She's a nice little thing in some ways, but obviously hopelessly spoilt by whoever brought her up. I shall have to speak to Nuray about it.'

'Today we are going to Perge,' Nuray announced, when the group had assembled outside the hotel's entrance. 'Perge was founded about a thousand years before Christ and was deliberately sited twenty kilometres inland to be safe from raids by the pirates who terrorised the coast. Now please board the truck and we'll get started.'

At Perge, Serif parked the truck outside the city's amphitheatre.

As she handed out tickets, Nuray said in her clear, carrying voice, 'The theatre could seat fourteen thousand people on forty-two levels. We'll climb to the top, where you'll be able to see what a large city this was.'

Nicola's admiration for the skills of the people who had designed and built the theatre was counterbalanced by the knowledge that their idea of entertainment had often included spectacles involving brutal slaughter.

Watching, from the arena, Richard's agile progress up the steps to the uppermost tiers, she didn't think that had he lived in those times he would have enjoyed the gladiatorial events. But perhaps he would have watched the slaves and other victims being butchered with an air of indifference if his career required it. She felt sure he would have been an achiever whatever age he had lived in.

I should have been a slave, she thought, with a wry smile.

As she climbed to the top, the steps being too high for her to leap up them as easily as he had, she found herself trying to reconcile her previous ideas about him with the impressions she was receiving on this trip.

The two didn't match, which made her feel confused and unsettled.

Although it was not yet mid-morning, the sun was sufficiently warm for everyone to start stripping down to their T-shirts.

As Nuray was allowing half an hour for them to explore the theatre and take photographs, Nicola wandered off by herself and sat down to bask in the sun.

She had emptied her mind of all thoughts and was luxuriating in a warmth not enjoyed since the previous summer when an unmistakable voice said, 'You must take care not to burn.'

'I put sun-filter on my face first thing this morning,' she said, opening her eyes to look up at Serif. 'Actually I tan quite easily. I'm not as fair-skinned as Sylvie.'

He sat down beside her. 'I've tried talking to her but she has nothing to say. She seems scared of me. Perhaps

someone has warned her that Turkish men may try to
seduce her.'

'Some of them might,' said Nicola.

'But not me. I don't make passes at nervous virgins.'

Nicola was inclined to doubt that Sylvie was as
innocent as he thought, even if most Turkish girls of her
age were.

She said, 'Surely, for you, it's not a good idea to make
passes at anyone? If they complained, you could find
yourself out of a job.'

'The women I make love to don't complain... they
enjoy it,' Serif said, with a grin. 'I'm a very good lover.'

'Most men think they're wonderful drivers and wonderful lovers. Some of them are, some of them aren't.'

'You sound as if you've had a lot of experience.'

'Very little. I'm going by things I've read in books and
magazines.' Then, hurriedly changing the subject, 'Don't
you get bored, visiting these places repeatedly?'

'Sometimes... if the people we're guiding are boring.
Then I stay in the truck and sleep... or write a poem.'

Nicola said, 'Turkish is a very musical language. I've
listened to you and Nuray talking and the sounds aren't
harsh to the ear like those of some languages.'

He slanted a teasing look at her. 'It sounds even better
when it's whispered in your ear on a warm night by the
sea. Perhaps one night soon I'll give you a demonstration.'

She said composedly, 'I'm sure everyone would like
to hear you recite one of your poems to us, Serif. I think
Nuray is signalling that it's time to move on.'

# CHAPTER FIVE

FROM the theatre they walked to Perge's large stadium and then to the entrance to the city.

Leading them to a pillared square with traces of mosaic pavements, Nuray said, 'This was the *agora* or market-place, surrounded by shops. There would have been more to see at the beginning of this century. Unfortunately in the 1920s there was a building boom in a village near here and Perge offered a good supply of stone.'

'Would you mind if I snapped you, Nuray?' Richard asked, as she finished speaking.

'You'll get a better shot if I stand here.' She moved closer to a pillar, the naturalness of her pose showing she was used to being photographed.

Today she had shed her dark overcoat and was in jeans and an apricot sweatshirt with a coral scarf. The colours flattered her olive skin. Standing beside the tall stone column with the blue sky as a background, she had a dramatic beauty. Everyone took a photograph of her.

From the market they followed a long paved street lined with columns before retracing their steps to look around the Roman baths where two of the original pools had been excavated.

'For the Romans, the baths were like London's famous gentlemen's clubs,' she told them.

Before the take-over which had put Richard in charge, the London office of Barking & Dollis had been seething with gossip and speculation. Someone had found out that he was a member of the exclusive Racquets Club in New York, the equally exclusive Travellers' Club in Paris, and also had the entrée to a bastion of the British Establishment.

64

This news put some people against him before they met him. Nicola remembered one of her colleagues—a bolshie type who begrudged anyone having anything he didn't have—whingeing about Richard's privileged background. At the time she had defended him, saying that the new chief executive might give the company a badly needed injection of American drive and efficiency. Never dreaming, as she spoke, that she would be among the first to feel his axe.

As Nuray pointed out the tunnels where warm air had circulated, Nicola found herself thinking that, even if Richard had come from a humble background, he would have been born to lead, not to follow, to command rather than obey.

The very way he stood was indicative. While Stuart leaned against a wall and Philip sat slumped on a convenient ledge, Richard's stance was relaxed but upright, one hand holding the strap of the light pack slung on his shoulder, the thumb of his other hand hooked through the braided leather belt round his lean waist.

She looked away before he could catch her staring at him.

'Now you can look around by yourselves. At twelve o'clock we'll meet at the truck and go for lunch,' said Nuray.

The group dispersed. Nicola wanted to photograph an unusually fine marble capital she had noticed lying on the grass near the baths, perhaps dislodged from its column by an earthquake.

Richard had the same idea. When she had taken her picture she found him standing near by.

'I like all my shots to have someone in them. Apart from adding interest, it shows the scale of the subject,' he said. 'Would you mind posing for me, Nicola?'

With less assurance than Nuray she moved to stand by the fallen capital.

'That's fine, but there's no need to look so serious. How about a smile?' He took two snaps in quick succession before closing the lens cover. 'Thanks.'

'Not at all.' She expected him to walk away but he seemed to be waiting for her to move and, when she did, fell into step beside her.

'If we had a time machine, we could take ourselves back to 333 BC when Alexander the Great was here. This must have been a magnificent city in its day. I'd like to see that colonnaded street by moonlight.'

Reminded of Serif's remark about Turkish being at its most musical when murmured in a girl's ear on a warm night, she wondered what Richard's voice would sound like in those circumstances.

'I'm sure Nuray would lay on some moonlit ruins for you, if you asked her,' she said lightly.

'She might... in the line of duty. I gather that Serif's offer was of a private nature. Just the two of you.'

She gave him a startled glance. How could he possibly know that? He had been on the other side of the amphitheatre when Serif had been talking to her. She remembered noticing Richard standing on the edge of a long drop and thinking he must have a better head for heights than she had.

He said drily, 'The acoustics in the theatre are excellent. Not only is it possible to hear everything said in the arena from the highest row of seats, but—depending on the wind, I imagine—private conversations between people on one side of the theatre can be heard on the other.'

'Oh... I see,' she said, disconcerted. Then, recovering her self-possession, 'So presumably you heard my answer... that we'd *all* like to hear him recite some of his poems.'

'I'm prepared to wait till his verses have appeared in print,' Richard answered. 'For me, amateur poetry recitals have as little appeal as Morris dancing. Anyway that's not what he had in mind. He'd prefer an audience of one.'

He had been surveying the ruins, but now he looked down at her.

'If I were you I'd steer clear of a secluded rendezvous with that guy. From what I've heard, the Turks have a low boiling point.'

'That might not be clear to Sylvie, but at twenty-six one does have a rough idea on how cope with the two-legged wolves of this world,' she said mildly.

'If you say so. But the wolves of Asia Minor may be harder to handle than the European species. Because this is an old-fashioned country where nice girls definitely don't, it doesn't follow that the men don't try their luck with foreigners.'

'I expect they do. And probably—sometimes—successfully. But I think Serif's bright enough to know who might fall for his line and who won't.'

'Don't count on it.'

They had lunch in a village bar where, as usual, only men were to be seen. The long table, spread with a plastic cloth, had been decorated with sprays of wild narcissi stuck in empty Coke bottles. Both Hilary and Nicola leaned forward to inhale their delicate fragrance.

'Did you notice the wild anemones growing in the ruins this morning, Nicola?' Hilary asked.

After lunch they went back to Antalya to see, on the outskirts of town, the Düden waterfall pouring over a cliff into the sea.

Richard looked faintly bored by this spectacle. He had probably seen Niagara and other more impressive falls, thought Nicola. Or perhaps he was beginning to regret taking his friend's place on a holiday which didn't provide either the standard of comfort he was accustomed to, or the high-powered people with whom he was used to mixing.

However their next stop, the Archaeological Museum, was good enough to satisfy the most exacting traveller.

'This is one of the best collections in Turkey,' Nuray told them. 'It's only a short walk back to our hotel and your time is free until we meet for dinner at seven. I have to shop for our picnic tomorrow so I'll leave you to enjoy the museum.'

The exhibit Nicola liked best was a dancer, larger than life-size, carved from two kinds of limestone, her face and body white marble, her hair and garments pale grey.

She had been badly damaged and her feet were missing, as were parts of her swirling draperies. But what had survived had been cleverly suspended in its correct position. Poised on a pedestal and lit by concealed spotlights, the statue recaptured all the lithe grace of the girl who had posed for an unknown but brilliant sculptor centuries before.

When Nicola returned to the entrance hall, more than an hour later, she seemed to be the only one of the group left in the museum. Then, through glass doors leading to a terrace and garden at the rear, she saw Richard and Janet sitting at a table, drinking coffee.

Rather than intrude, she bought some postcards of the dancer, and left. This was evidently a time of day when the well-heeled young of Antalya met for soft drinks at the cafés along the esplanade. Most of the girls wore jeans and the sexes seemed to mix as freely as they did in Europe, she noticed.

Instead of going back to the hotel, she continued walking to the centre of the town. After wandering through a maze of narrow streets lined with shops selling gold jewellery, leather goods and cheap holiday clothes, she stopped at a stall displaying the blue beads thought to ward off misfortune. For the equivalent of fifty pence, she bought ten medium-sized beads as an inexpensive souvenir.

She wouldn't have been here at all if it hadn't been for the generosity of her godmother. Every year Aunt

Ruth—who was actually a schoolfriend of her mother's, not a relation—gave her an extravagant Christmas present. Two years ago it had been a desktop PC, last year a food processor and a course of aromotherapy treatments. This year it had been a holiday. Aunt Ruth had picked out five holidays she thought her god-daughter would enjoy, leaving the final choice to Nicola.

She had chosen the trek in Turkey mainly because it didn't conflict with the culmination of a very important spare-time project she was involved with. Also she hoped it would have a tonic effect on her vitality at the low point of the winter, and erase from her mind the last vestige of negative feeling about the past. Physically it had already done her good. Emotionally, because of Richard's presence, it had had the opposite effect.

That night the group dined at a large *restoran* near the harbour. Among the other diners, only two had their wives with them. The rest of the tables were occupied by groups of men.

The meal began with the appetisers known as *mezes* including a creamy yogurt and cucumber dip.

Serif, at one end of the table, was drinking his usual *raki*.

Richard had ordered wine. When his glass had been filled, he raised it in Serif's direction and said, '*Serefe*!'

'Is that the Turkish equivalent of cheers?' Miles asked.

'So I gather,' said Richard. 'Although literally it means "to honour"... is that correct, Serif?'

The Turk nodded. 'But this is the way you should do it.'

He picked up his *raki* with a finger and thumb on the rim of the glass, swung it casually over his left shoulder, passed it behind his head and then, bringing it forward, upside-down, over his right shoulder, replaced it on the table.

The main course tonight was a meat stew accompanied by boiled cracked wheat to soak up the juices.

'Tomorrow we're going for a long hike, so tonight you must eat well, Sylvie. You'll need a lot of energy,' Serif told her, as she poked at the chunks of meat.

'I never eat much.'

'That's why you're too thin.'

'I'm not thin...I'm slim,' she protested. 'I don't want to be fat.'

'A little more flesh on your body would be an improvement,' he told her. 'Didn't you think the statues in the museum were beautiful women?'

She pulled one of her schoolgirlish faces. 'No, I didn't! Their hips were *huge*.'

'Only compared with the hips of model girls, and what use are they, except for showing off clothes? A woman should be built for making love and having babies.' The twinkle in Serif's showed he knew it was a provocative opinion. 'You agree, don't you, Richard? And Stuart?'

'You wouldn't get away with a statement like that in the UK,' Stuart told him. 'Or in the States. The feminists would have your guts for garters. Isn't that right, Rick?'

If Richard disliked being called Rick, he gave no sign. 'Said in all seriousness, yes, probably it would cause offence. But for my taste the statue of the dancer has as much appeal now as when it was sculpted.'

There was a chorus of assent, although Sylvie's puzzled expression suggested she had passed the dancer without noticing her.

For their pudding Nuray had ordered *kadayif*, a confection which looked like fine shredded wheat, drenched in a thick honey syrup.

After dinner they all went for a stroll round the marina. With nightfall the temperature had dropped. Even when they couldn't be seen, the proximity of snow-clad mountains could be felt in the razor-sharp air. Nicola was glad of the soft cashmere muffler her mother had given her last Christmas and the knitted gloves she had bought in a London street market.

In a café they ordered drinks and practised the glass-whirling toast Serif had shown them earlier. Predictably, Richard was the quickest to master the trick of doing it without any spills.

'This is only our fourth night in Turkey. It seems far longer than that since I left home,' said Janet when, with varying degrees of success, everyone had made two or three attempts to emulate Serif's skill.

She was looking at Richard as she spoke, but it was Nuray who answered.

'It's always the same. When I meet a new group at the airport, they're not very friendly. But it doesn't take long, on a trek, for them to become friends.'

'Sometimes lovers,' Serif tacked on, his dark gaze shifting from Janet to Nicola to Sylvie before returning to Nuray's face.

What that brief survey signified Nicola wasn't sure. But she saw that it didn't please the Turkish girl.

'That's not good,' Nuray said briskly. 'Most holiday romances don't last. Abroad, people are not the same as at home. They're on their best behaviour. To love someone truly you must know them as they really are.'

Next day, after a bumpy ride along dirt tracks used by forestry workers, Serif brought the truck to a halt on a bluff overlooking a river where minerals made the water the colour of a peacock's neck feathers.

'We will walk through Köprülü canyon and Serif will drive to the shepherd's house where we'll have tea,' Nuray told them. 'All this is national park.' Her gesture embraced a long range of soaring crags, their slopes dark with evergreen forest.

After skirting the river for about half an hour, they came to some widely spaced stepping stones to the far bank.

Nicola and Hilary managed these easily, as did the men, but Lorna and Sylvie would have slipped and fallen if they hadn't been helped. Philip also lost his balance, reaching the other side with his trainers squelching water.

'That guy's on the wrong vacation. He should be in Miami or Torremolinos,' Richard said in a low-voiced aside to Hilary which Nicola overheard.

For a reason she couldn't analyse, she found herself saying, rather acidly, 'Not everyone can be Superman. Maybe he's not such a wimp as you seem to think.'

They both turned to look at her; Hilary with a faintly surprised smile, Richard with an ironical lift of the eyebrow.

'Fallen for him, Nicola?' he asked, in an amused voice.

Ignoring the quip, she said, 'Snap judgements can be wrong. I need to know people well before I decide they're worthless.'

'I don't think Richard intended to write Philip off,' Hilary said, in a placatory tone. 'But he certainly isn't equipped for this type of holiday. Nor is Sylvie.'

Richard laughed. 'That little thing isn't equipped to grapple with any eventualities. But I guess there'll always be someone around to rescue her.'

Hilary said, 'I often wish I had learned to play the helpless female when I was young instead of being trained to be sensible and capable in an era when far fewer women stood on their own feet. Today the pendulum has swung too far. Many thoroughly feminine females feel obliged to pretend they aren't. Would you agree, Nicola?'

'In what way?' said Nicola, wishing she hadn't sprung to Philip's defence. If anyone other than Richard had made that remark about him, she would have smiled agreement. It *was* hard to fathom why Philip had chosen this holiday. But Richard's disparaging comment had reminded her of his assessment of her own capabilities and prompted that foolishly pointed gibe about Superman.

'Take Lorna, for example,' said Hilary, after casting an eye behind her to make sure Lorna and Stuart were well out of earshot. 'In my day, she'd have travelled with a girlfriend, not a young man. Is that freedom really to her advantage? They're obviously having disagreements. When they get home the relationship will probably end. What will Lorna have gained by shaking off the restraints in force in her mother's and aunts' youth? Experience, yes—but at the price of disillusionment.'

She was walking alongside Nicola now, with Richard following close behind. It was he who, when Nicola remained silent, considering her reply, said, 'Isn't it better for them to find out now that they don't suit each other than on what, in an earlier era, would have been their honeymoon?'

'It's the argument usually advanced in favour of the present system,' the older woman answered. 'I'm not convinced. An incontrovertible fact is that any two people of the opposite sex are going to have problems adjusting to living together. If Stuart and Lorna *were* on their honeymoon, they would be more careful of each other's feelings. They would both take a different attitude simply because they were in an ongoing situation.'

'Any couple who chose a group trek for their honeymoon would need their heads examined,' said Richard.

Hilary laughed. 'Definitely! Although having a "structured honeymoon"—one with something to do other than making love—is a good idea. That's why, in my day, touring honeymoons were popular.'

He said, 'You're keeping very quiet, Nicola. Do you agree with Hilary?'

'I agree that Lorna would have enjoyed this trip more without Stuart as her partner.'

'That's side-stepping. We want to know where you stand on the question of unmarried people taking holidays together.'

'You haven't said where you stand,' she pointed out.

'That goes without saying...he's in favour,' Hilary answered for him. 'Most men are—except the fathers of daughters. Their views tend to be stricter. As far as young unattached men are concerned, the present moral climate is a dream come true.' She cast a teasing glance upwards at the man behind her. 'Isn't that so?'

'You could say that,' he agreed. 'But women must like it or they wouldn't go along with it. In the old days manners and mores were dictated by my sex. Not any more...at least not in the western world. You may not approve of the ways things are, Hilary, but Nicola's generation does. They still have the option to keep us at arm's length, but they don't choose to exercise it.'

'Men have never been kept at arm's length by women in love,' said Hilary. 'Not unless they were extremely closely chaperoned. Even when I was young, nice girls did...given the opportunity. But usually, if not invariably, for love. Not casually, as they do now. Not simply to be in the swing. That's what I find sad...the absence of passionate feeling in so many relationships. But of course that's the view of a spinster *d'un certain âge* and I don't expect you to share it.'

Had they been alone, Nicola would have surprised her by agreeing. But this wasn't a subject she wanted to discuss with Richard listening in.

'I don't think age or status have much to do with the validity of people's views,' he said to Hilary. 'If you were a teacher, dealing with parents as well as children, you must know a lot about human relationships.'

'I've certainly seen the pain that the failure of their parents' marriages inflicts on children,' she answered. 'Dear me, what a depressing subject for a lovely day. I'm most interested in your *métier*, Richard. Although I'm an avid reader, I know very little about publishing. What made you choose it as a career?'

'My grandfather was a publisher and my father started out as one but then changed to politics. It was expected of me.'

'Would you rather have done something else?' she asked.

'If I had, I would have done it. No, I was happy to conform to family tradition. I wouldn't be where I am now—in charge of a major imprint—if I hadn't had that background. It might have taken another ten years to get there...ten years I can be using to push through much needed reforms.'

Nicola wanted very much to hear this conversation. At the same time she knew it was risky. Any discussion of publishing increased the likelihood that her name and face would suddenly ring a bell with him.

'What reforms?' asked Hilary.

'Half the girls in publishing—and it's currently a predominantly female occupation except at the highest levels—haven't had any serious training,' he explained. 'They've picked up what they need to know, or picked up some but not all the necessary knowledge. Now steps are being taken to improve our training system.'

'If the donkey work is done by women, why aren't they reaching the top places?' Hilary asked.

'I thought they were,' said Nicola. Knowing it was probably unwise, she cited the four who had been her role models, and another who, since she had lost her own job, had broken through the so-called glass ceiling to become a chief executive.

'A few have done very well,' he conceded. 'But you're talking about a handful of exceptional women and there's still a long way to go before we see a woman heading the Publishers' Association.'

Nicola had heard it said that, in spite of being only half-British, he was in line for that distinction and might become the youngest publisher ever to be so honoured.

'I'm sorry...I've taken the wrong path,' said Nuray. 'I think it's best we go back to where I made the mistake.'

'Oh, no!' The protest came from Sylvie. 'How far is that?'

'Two or three kilometres, not more.'

Sylvie groaned. 'What's that in miles?' Her voice had the petulant whine of a fractious child.

'What makes you think this isn't the right path, Nuray?' asked Richard.

'If it were, we should be at the shepherd's house now. There's no sign of a house.'

'Have a rest-stop while Miles and I do some scouting,' he suggested. 'From the top of that rising ground, we may be able to get our bearings.'

'How come you don't know the way?' Lorna asked, when the two men had set off together.

'I've only done this walk once before. Last time, I had a bad cold and Serif led the walk through the canyon while I stayed at the shepherd's house. I'm very sorry.'

'It doesn't matter, dear,' said Joan. 'It won't be dark for a long time yet. If the worst comes to the worst, we can go back to he beginning and wait there till Serif comes to find us.'

'That's *miles* back. We'd be exhausted,' Lorna said grumpily.

'If you thought coming over the mountains with a broken heater was cold, wait till you've spent a night in the open,' said Bob.

His tone was jovial and raised a supportive laugh from his wife, Hilary and Nicola. But Sylvie looked ready to burst into tears.

'There may be bears...or wolves.' She looked nervously round her.

'Not in this part of Turkey,' Hilary said firmly. 'And the men would light a fire for us. It would be an adventure.'

Nuray looked gratefully at her. She was obviously deeply embarrassed and perhaps was worrying about the complaints some of the party might make to her employers.

'No joy. We'd better go back to the point where Nuray thinks we went wrong,' said Richard, when he came back.

'Where *she* went wrong,' Lorna muttered.

'It's easy to make a mistake when the paths through the wooded areas look so much alike.' He gave Nuray a charming smile.

The Turkish girl's anxious frown cleared.

The effect of his smile on Nicola was known only to herself, and did nothing for her peace of mind. If she could react to a smile which wasn't even directed at her, what would happen if it were? she wondered.

I will *not* be attracted to him, she told herself resolutely.

But as the group began to retrace their footsteps, some with a good grace, others with sulky expressions, she knew it was already too late.

She had been attracted to Richard Russell from the moment she had walked into his office. Which somehow had made the ensuing interview even more galling than if he had been the kind of man with thinning hair and thickening waistline more commonly found in the seats of power.

Watching his tall erect figure as he walked with Nuray at the head of the column, she thought no one would ever guess the taut and sexy backside outlined by his blue jeans spent a lot of time chair-bound. Dressed as he was, in this setting, he looked the quintessential out-doors man; every line of his body designed for strenuous action.

Stop thinking about the man, will you? she told herself impatiently. You're becoming obsessed with him.

# CHAPTER SIX

IT WAS late afternoon when a herd of long-haired black goats appeared, followed by a prune-faced crone in a headscarf and Turkish trousers. A long machete-style knife was stuck through the back of the cloth wrapped round her waist.

She and Nuray greeted each other with relief on the Turkish girl's side and much toothless laughter from the goat-keeper.

'Don't fraternise with the goats,' Miles remarked, as the animals surrounded them, chewing tasty mouthfuls from the undergrowth and eyeing the strangers with calm curiosity. 'Those white things in the partings along their spines are ticks.'

Janet gave a dramatic shudder. 'What a life for the poor old thing! Living miles from anywhere with only goats for company. Thank God I wasn't born in rural Turkey.'

'She looks happy enough,' said Miles, as another cackle of laughter echoed through the woods.

'We're nearly there now,' said Nuray. 'Soon you'll be able to rest and have tea.'

'Looking at our hostess's hands, I'm not sure I want to take tea with her,' murmured Janet.

The house which came into view about ten minutes later was not the picturesque hovel they had expected. It was in the process of being rebuilt with bricks, perhaps with money sent back from Germany or Italy by immigrant sons.

On a crude wooden balcony giving access to rooms on the upper floor, Serif was asleep. As the group approached, a girl emerged from a room on the ground floor and called up to him. By the time Nuray was within speaking distance, he was on his feet, looking down at the weary walkers.

'Like a panther on a sunny branch,' Hilary remarked to Janet and Nicola.

Rather an apt analogy, thought Nicola. Showing his white teeth in a yawn, raking his fingers through his lustrous black hair and then stretching his muscular arms, Serif did bring to mind that sinuous and predatory member of the cat family.

'What kept you?' he asked. 'You're late.'

'We took a wrong turn,' Richard told him.

To which Nuray added, 'I lost the way. Never mind, we're here now. Come down and help serve the tea.'

'Aysel will do it.' Serif leaned over the balcony and spoke to the other Turkish girl.

'She looks like the cat that swallowed the canary,' said Janet. 'My guess is that, while granny was out with the goats, there've been fun and games here. The girl's very pretty. Can you see Serif wasting an opportunity like that?'

Nicola took her glass of sweet tea to a wooden platform built out over a slope which appeared to be where the family would sit in summer. It had a magnificent upward view of soaring rose-red cliffs.

'Are you tired?' Serif asked, coming to join her. Instead of looking at the view, he lounged on the rail surrounding the platform, looking at her.

'A little. But it's been a good day. This is a wonderful country.'

'Would you like to live here?'

She shook her head. 'It's too remote for me. Do you know how old the goat-lady is?'

He shrugged. 'Forty-five... fifty.'

'She looks seventy.'

'It's a hard life without electricity. All the water has to be carried to the house in buckets. Before her son went abroad, they were very poor. Now it's a little better but they still don't live the way you do.' He reached out and touched her cheek with the back of his knuckles. 'Your skin will never be like old dry leather.'

'I hope not.' She wondered how many tourists had felt that tender gesture and been told the same thing.

Serif's eyes switched from her face to a point somewhere behind her.

'We are under observation,' he murmured. 'Richard is a typical Englishman, isn't he?'

She glanced over her shoulder. Richard was standing by the corner of the house. His sunglasses made it impossible to tell if he was watching them or admiring the view.

'Actually he's an American with an English mother. Why does he strike you as being typically English?' she asked.

'The English are suspicious of foreigners, especially of foreign men who look admiringly at their women. They're also snobs. A Turkish truck driver isn't good enough to touch the cheek of an English young lady. That's what he's thinking.'

'He's far more likely to be wishing he could climb those cliffs. You're talking about Englishmen the way some of them were fifty years ago. Now we're part of the European Community and Richard himself is exceptionally cosmopolitan.'

'You're very quick to defend him. Perhaps you like him better than you like me.'

'Actually I would just as soon this were an all-women trek,' she told him, hoping to take the wind out of his sails. 'Mixed groups aren't as relaxing as a single-sex expeditions.'

Serif looked perplexed. 'Are you saying that you find women more attractive than men?'

'Not in the sense you mean. But I enjoy the company of other women, if they're intelligent and interesting. Men are happy in the company of other men. Why shouldn't we be content with our own sex?'

He disconcerted her by saying shrewdly, 'I think a man has hurt you and now you are nervous in case it happens again.'

There was an element of truth in his diagnosis. She had been bitterly hurt by Ian's reaction to her dismissal. But that was a long time ago and she wasn't aware of backing away from new relationships for fear they might turn out badly. There was always an element of risk in loving people. She knew that and accepted it.

'I'd like some more tea, if it's possible,' she said, handing him her glass.

'Of course.'

'Without sugar, please?'

He went off to fetch it and, instead of waiting for him as he probably expected her to, Nicola took the opportunity to rejoin the others.

As they were saying goodbye to the herdswoman, the old lady suddenly plunged her hand inside the collar of Janet's shirt. Pulling out a gold chain, she examined it closely before giving a nod of approval and stuffing it back in place, at the same time making a remark to Nuray.

'What did she say?' asked Janet.

'She's never seen a gold necklace as thick as yours. She thinks you must have a very rich husband.'

'If only I had,' was Janet's laughing comment.

When Nicola shook hands and said, '*Tesekkür*,' she was surprised to receive a kiss on both cheeks.

'I wish we had thought to bring a small present for her,' she said to Nuray.

'We provided the tea and sugar. There's plenty left over. She's satisfied.'

Although the next day was hot, they arrived at the beach to find it almost deserted; a mile or two of clean pale sand washed by a sparkling sea with some ruins among the wooded cliffs at the eastern end. Some upturned boats made convenient backrests.

Hilary was the first to test the temperature of the water by paddling.

'Invigorating!' she reported.

'Does that mean freezing?' Janet asked suspiciously.

'No, no...just a bit cold at first.' Hilary started to undress.

Richard had already stripped off his shirt.

'That's an expensive tan,' murmured Janet, watching him unzip his jeans.

As he took them off, revealing dark boxer-style swim shorts, powerful muscles rippled under the silky brown skin of his back and shoulders. Bob, who was changing near him, had long lost the lean elasticity which characterised Richard's physique.

They were all in the sea, Richard far out in the deep water and the rest closer to the shore, when Serif came sprinting down the beach in a brief red slip and kicked up a froth of spray before taking a running header.

He surfaced close to Nicola, his thick curls momentarily flattened before a quick flick of his head restored their springiness.

Neither Nuray nor Philip joined the swimmers, and the others had been out of the water for quarter of an hour before Richard waded ashore after his more vigorous exertions.

'An interesting contrast, those two,' said Janet, watching him talking to Serif while she and Nicola applied sun-cream. 'Quite alike in some ways and totally different in others. Which one do you prefer?'

'I don't know,' said Nicola. 'Which do you?'

'Both of them could be hard to handle. Perhaps Miles would be the best bet. Older men are more restful.'

Janet leaned back on her elbows. She had changed into another swimsuit, a red one with high-cut legs and a top which stayed up without straps.

'Sometimes I wonder if men are worth all the hassle. Hilary's managed without one and doesn't seem unhappy about it.'

Nicola's gaze returned to the two men standing with their backs to the sea and their eyes on the wooded hinterland. Now that they had no clothes on, or none that disguised their conformation, it was clear that Richard's extra two inches were in the length of his legs, which were also less hairy than Serif's.

Both had impressive shoulders but, while Serif's chest had a breastplate of coarse black hair tapering down past his navel, Richard's chest had the polished smoothness of the marble gods in the museum.

Janet was lying down, oblivious of everything but the heat of the sun on her supine body. Nicola followed her example, trying to concentrate on the soft sound of the waves brushing the beach a few yards away, and what Nuray's promised surprise for the afternoon might be.

But sunbathing was not a good way to clear the mind of erotic fancies, she found. A few moments later she sat up, reached for her shirt, and set off along the beach.

On the way back, strolling by the water's edge, she saw Richard loping towards her at a lazy run.

He slowed down as they came abreast.

'Did you enjoy your swim?'

'Very much. You obviously enjoyed yours.'

'Being desk-bound a lot of the time, I need all the exercise I can get. This trip isn't as strenuous as I'd hoped. Is it turning out as you expected?'

'More or less . . . except I thought there'd be more of us, including one or two Aussies and other nationalities.'

She thought he had stopped to talk to her out of politeness and would soon continue his run.

Instead he said, 'It's close to lunchtime. I'd better turn back with you. Tell me about your job at Chatham's.'

'Like Gertrude Stein's rose, a secretary is a secretary is a secretary.'

He swooped to pick up a piece of sea-polished glass. 'I often think secretaries are the only essential species in the entire business world.'

'Perhaps less essential than they used to be in these days of lap-tops and modems and personal organisers,' said Nicola.

'It's still mainly the travelling salesmen who use those aids. It's amazing how many top-level people are computer illiterates. I don't think the efficient secretary is in any danger of extinction...and I'm sure you're very efficient.'

'What makes you think so?'

'I noticed you checking the slip when you changed currency at the airport. You don't have to rummage for your passport when we check in at hotels. You're the only one who says please and thank you in Turkish. You file the illustrated tickets Nuray hands out in your guide-book.'

It was disconcerting to find she had been under close observation. But perhaps he had studied the others equally closely.

'You seem to have missed your vocation,' she said lightly. 'With your eye for clues to character, you should have been a detective.'

He laughed. 'Maybe I should. My favourite light reading is crime fiction. Do you read crime novels?'

'Sometimes. As you said you were interested in history, I'd have thought that would be your main reading.'

'It is. The crime stuff is for unwinding.'

She knew it was risky, but she couldn't resist asking, 'Do you need much unwinding? I thought Barking & Dollis were over the difficulties they had a few years ago.'

'We are. If you talk to people who've been in the book trade a long time—any business, come to that—they'll tell you that booms and busts come and go like the seasons and the weather. Been with Chatham's long?'

'Yes.' She left it at that.

'You must know our central London rep... George Morden.'

She nodded. George Morden wasn't aware she had once worked for his employers. He had joined Barking & Dollis soon after she left them, head-hunted by the man strolling beside her.

'He's the tops,' Richard said. 'It's a key job and I wanted the best man in it so I poached him from one of our rivals.'

'I gather you have a reputation for ruthlessness.'

'I have? Where have you heard that? Not from George?'

It was interesting that he called the rep by his first name. His predecessor, a publisher of the old school, had referred to the sales force by their surnames.

'No, he's loud in your praise. I've heard him telling my boss that you're the best thing that's happened to British publishing in years.'

He laughed. 'That's because I pay him more than he was getting before. Also it's part of his spiel to make people believe B & D is being run by a genius. The average book buyer doesn't know or care who a book is published by, but presumably in your job you do notice the colophon on a book you've enjoyed? What do you think of our list?'

'It's excellent,' she said truthfully. It was on the tip of her tongue to add, But presumably that's because you have some of the best commissioning editors in the business.

She repressed the comment. This conversation was already skating dangerously close to a confrontation which could only result in mutual embarrassment for the rest of the holiday.

'That's good to hear,' he said, smiling at her. 'Not that I can take much of the credit, except in the sense that authors are attracted to a publishing house where they're likely to get a fair deal and be treated in a civilised way. Most of the kudos must go to our editors.'

To steer the conversation away from editors, Nicola said, 'George Morden says your campaign against the sale-or-return system is the most important change you want to make.'

It was clearly a subject on which he had strong views. He shared them with her for several minutes before breaking off to say, 'Sorry, you didn't come on holiday to hear me riding my hobby-horse. Let's talk about cookery. What sort of things do you like to cook?'

'I'm a Sunday supplement cook. Most of the recipes I try out are clipped from the weekend papers. I learnt the basics from my mother when I was small.'

'It sounds as if you had one of those nice old-fashioned happy family childhoods that are supposed to be dying out.'

'Yes, I did. Didn't you?'

'My parents didn't get on too well. Their relationship is largely a front for my father's political career. My mother is English. When she went to live in the States, she took with her the person we call Nan who had been her nurse as a child. Nan looked after us as well . . . us being myself, my two brothers and my sister. She gave us the cosy home background while our parents were busy politicking and socialising. So, like you, I had a good childhood but in a different way. Do you see much of your parents now?'

'About every third weekend. They're only forty-five minutes away.'

'Is that by car or train?'

'Train. I have a driving licence and Dad lets me use his car, but there would be no point in my keeping one in London. Do you?'

He nodded. 'I spend quite a few weekends with my English grandparents. They live in Wiltshire. It would be an awkward journey by public transport. Do you know that part of England?'

When she shook her head, he went on, 'It's peaceful down there. Nothing has changed much since my grandfather was my age. It's a great place for recharging one's batteries.'

Lord Rotherhithe's gardens were said to be among the most beautiful in Britain, a fitting setting for a Tudor mansion owned by the same family for centuries. But the way Richard referred to it, it might have been a sequestered country cottage. In an age when many people lost no chance to show off, she couldn't help liking the way he played down his background.

By this time they were back with the others who were preparing to go to the *lotanka* behind the beach for lunch.

'What's on the menu today, Nuray?'

'Not a big choice today, Bob. Tomato soup, salad, spaghetti and chips. Is that all right for you?'

'Sounds fine to me,' he beamed.

'Spaghetti *and* chips!' murmured Janet, as she and Nicola pulled on their trousers. 'And bread too, no doubt. I can't take all this carbohydrate they're pushing into us.'

'Have the soup and salad and pass on the rest,' Nicola suggested.

They ate at a table outside the *lotanka* served by a smiling woman in Turkish trousers with a clean white cotton headscarf covering her hair and tied at the nape of her neck.

The beautiful setting, the toned-up feeling left by her swim and the expectation of an interesting afternoon combined to give Nicola a strong sense of well-being. There was only one fly in the ointment—Richard. And the disturbing change in her feelings towards him.

How could she be warming towards someone who had done what he had done, not only to her but to other people? It had been the act of a despot, a man to whom other people were merely pawns in the power game. There must have been a way to put the company back on its feet without all those arbitrary dismissals.

After lunch Nuray said, 'Now you can rest or swim again until four o'clock. Then we're going for a walk to see something very unusual. Those of you who have torches should bring them.'

'We're not going caving, are we?' asked Janet. 'If so, count me out. I'm claustrophobic.'

Nuray shook her head. 'But it will be dark when we come down the mountain. The track is good but a torch will be an advantage.'

Nicola decided to combine a sunbathe with writing a letter to her friend Gina Latimer. Whether the letter would reach London before Nicola did was debatable, but it would relieve her feelings to tell Gina about Richard being here.

Gina was another victim of the recession. She had worked in the PR side of publishing and now had a job in the customer relations department of a major chain store. But she found it dull compared with writing Press releases, organising author tours and liaising with the media.

Together they were involved in an enterprise they hoped would triumphantly redress their set-backs. Gina had jumped at the proposition Nicola had put to her and they had spent the past nine months giving most of their spare time to it.

Very soon their labours would bear fruit. If they pulled it off, the success of their venture would prove that both Richard Russell and the man who had laid off Gina had made a mistake as classic as that of the several publishers who had turned down the chance to buy Frederick Forsyth's massively successful book *The Day of the Jackal*.

Of course, they might *not* pull it off. But after a lot of discussion they had felt it was a risk worth taking.

If their hopes were fulfilled, Nicola knew that nothing in her life would ever give her greater satisfaction than proving Richard Russell wrong.

Dear Gina,
    You'll never guess who's here. My No. 1 *bête noire*! He has no idea who I am. At first I thought he might

be pretending not to recognise me, but now I think it's genuine. If I didn't know what a heartless pig he can be, I might succumb to his charm, which is considerable.

I'm writing this at the beach. Later we're going on a mystery tour up a mountain, led by our Turkish guide. She seems to be boss of our outfit—though I don't think the driver likes it when she tells him what to do—but from what I've seen so far the majority of Turkish women have a long way to go to equality.

Although it's good to relax after the long hard slog of the past few months, my mind is still mainly on The Project. I can't wait for blast-off...

The track wound its way through a pine wood and then skirted a ravine, twisting and turning among outcrops of limestone and fir trees. It was an easy climb which soon had them high above sea-level.

Presently Nuray called a halt, suggesting they make themselves comfortable on flat-topped rocks.

'Some of you will have heard of the Lycian hero Bellerophon and his winged horse, Pegasus. For a long time this part of the Lycian kingdom had been terrorised by the Chimera, a fire-breathing monster with a lion's head, a goat's body and a serpent's tail.'

As she spoke, her dark eyes ranged over the group. But it seemed to Nicola that the one she looked at most often was Richard.

'The King of Lycia sent Bellerophon to kill the monster,' Nuray went on. 'Because he could fly out of its reach on Pegasus, he succeeded. According to legend, it happened higher up this mountain, and the fire from the monster's dying breath is still burning under the rocks. In a few moments you'll see the flames.'

By now it was growing dusk. They seemed a long way from the nearest human habitation as they pressed on up the track to an open space where no trees were growing. At the foot of this expanse of bare rock was a

small cluster of ruins. The air had a strange, rather unpleasant smell.

'Methane,' said Richard. 'What used to be called
marsh gas or, in coal mines, fire-damp.'

'I thought fire-damp was dangerous,' said Janet.

'It's explosive when it's mixed with air and comes into
contact with naked flame. But only in confined spaces.'

'The fires show up better in the dark,' said Serif.

He had a dry piece of brushwood in his hand. When
he held it to the flames coming from a hole in the rock
it caught alight and he was able to ignite escapes of gas
from other holes.

'Be careful where you sit down,' he told the trekkers.
'Some people find the smell makes them feel sick.'

'I don't like this place. It's creepy,' said Sylvie, looking
round as if she expected to see the fire-snarling Chimera
burst from the rocks to devour them.

'In ancient times it was thought to be a holy place,'
said Nuray. 'Now, in summer, it's a popular picnic spot.
You can see the ashes of fires where people have cooked
food.'

By the time it was fully dark, Serif had piled
brushwood near several vents and soon he had three large
fires going, their flames casting a flickering red glow over
the ruins and the faces of the trekkers.

'I think we must leave now,' said Nuray, as the blaze
began to die down. 'By the time we reach Finike and get
settled in our new rooms, it will be time for supper.'

Apart from Sylvie and Philip, everyone had a torch
to use where the trees were thick and their branches cast
dense shadows. Where there were fewer trees, moonlight
and starlight lit the way.

They set out in a crocodile but because some of the
group were more sure-footed than others the file became
more and more strung out. Soon Nuray, who was
leading, could no longer be heard talking to Miles who
was behind her.

Nicola was held up by Bob and Joan plodding cautiously down in front of her. Joan seemed particularly unsure of herself in the dark, but she didn't suggest Nicola should pass her. Perhaps she found it reassuring to have two people behind to help Bob pick her up if she missed her footing.

The last in the line was Serif, who had given the truck's keys to Nuray so that the first down wouldn't have to wait for the last-comers.

They were about halfway when Nicola heard a noise which made her check and turn. It had sounded like a thud followed by a muffled expletive.

She waited for the beam of Serif's torch to appear round the outcrop she had passed a few moments earlier. When it didn't, she wondered if he could have slipped and fallen. It didn't seem likely. He had a powerful torch and was light on his feet.

'Serif?'

When there was no reply to her call, she turned back and went round the great rock.

'*Serif*!'

He was sprawled at full length on the path.

What could have happened to knock him out? she wondered, going down on her knees beside him and shining her torch on his unconscious face.

She was drawing in her breath to give loud yell for help when his eyes opened. With a big grin, he sat up and put both arms round her.

'Did you think the Chimera had got me?'

'Oh, Serif... that isn't funny,' she protested. 'You're too old to play such a trick.'

'I was bored. Bob and Joan go so slowly. We can soon catch them up.'

As she tried to disengage herself, he pulled her closer and kissed her. It was only a light, playful kiss and he didn't attempt to prolong it.

'There! Wasn't that nice?' he asked softly.

It was hard to deny that being kissed by a good-looking man, especially after a prolonged dearth of kisses, *was* rather nice.

Taking her hesitation for assent, he said, 'Let's do it again.'

This time the pressure of his lips was firmer and she felt the rasp of his five o'clock shadow against her chin. But when his arms moved and he tried to hold her more closely, she resisted and struggled free.

'The others will think we've *both* been seized by the Chimera,' she said rather breathlessly. 'Come on; we must catch them up.'

He let her go and together they scrambled to their feet.

'Later...' he said. 'Later there'll be time to be together.'

Nicola let that pass. She started to hurry down the track, resolved not to fall for any more of his strategies.

'Be careful. You're going too fast,' he warned her.

She slowed slightly, wondering if Joan had noticed they were no longer close behind her. If they didn't get back to the truck at the same time as the Tufnells, it would be typical of Joan to say archly, 'What happened to you two?'

In fact she needn't have worried. Very soon she saw Joan's light ahead and the other woman didn't seem aware that the last two in the line had fallen behind for a while.

In the truck Janet was retouching her lipstick. As she settled in the seat opposite, Nicola was glad her own lips were bare. Had Serif kissed Janet, there would have been tell-tale smudges round both their mouths.

On the run to their next destination she thought about his kisses and about tactful ways to explain he was wasting his time.

Casual sex—which presumably was his objective—had never appealed to her. She believed a prerequisite of making love was feelings of genuine affection and tenderness, not just a strong physical attraction.

After the break-up with Ian, she had decided that love was a snare and a delusion. She wasn't even sure any longer that she wanted to marry and have children.

Her parents were happily married, as were most of their friends. But somehow, between her parents' generation and her own, the ability to pick the right partner and stay married for life seemed almost to have died out. Among her own circle—made up mainly of former and current colleagues—most were either living together, or separated, or second-time-around.

It was all very well for her mother to insist that true love and a life of happiness 'till death us do part' was still a viable concept. Gina, after two abortive relationships, had given up waiting for Mr Wonderful to materialise.

'Mr Dull Steady DIY-Expert is the guy I'm looking for now,' she had said once. 'Or if I do fall in love again, I'll go into it with my eyes open, knowing it won't last.'

Nicola had ageed. Yet tucked away in a corner of her heart was the tenacious longing to meet a man and live 'happily ever after'. Not just on a humdrum level of mutual convenience and tolerance, but in Shakespeare's marriage of true minds.

# CHAPTER SEVEN

'TONIGHT, Sylvie, you're sharing with Nicola,' said Nuray, in the lobby of the hotel at Finike.

Nicola soon discovered for herself why Hilary had disliked sharing with the youngest member of the group. Sylvie's method of unpacking was to unload the confusion in her kitbag on to her bed and then lay claim to most of the room's inadequate storage space.

'You can have first go in the shower, if you like,' she said, dumping a jumble of cosmetics on the table between the two beds.

Nicola jumped at the offer, foreseeing that Sylvie would leave the bathroom a mess. To her dismay there was no hot water.

Feeling sticky from her swim, she forced herself to have a cold shower. Although they had been warned that hot water might not always be available, its absence came hard to anyone accustomed to an unfailing supply. But the cold shower made her feel good afterwards.

'I'm not going to torture myself,' said Sylvie, when Nicola emerged. 'I've been in the sea today. I wonder if there's a disco here? The evenings are *boring*!'

'Ask Serif. He looks like a night owl.'

'He's too old for me,' said Sylvie. 'Still, better than no one, I s'pose. I thought there'd be lots of good-looking Turkish waiters. My friend had a great time last summer.'

They ate at a restaurant on the outskirts of town, a great barn of a place which, in season, could cater for several hundred tourists. Tonight the only diners were the Amazing Adventures group and, at a smaller table, four men who looked like travelling salesmen.

The long table set for the group was lit by night-lights inside flowers made from thinly cut curls of orange peel. They cast a flattering golden glow on the diners' faces.

'It's a pity there's no one of Sylvie's age on this trek,' Nicola said to Nuray, as the meal began with an excellent thyme and pea soup.

The Turkish girl nodded. 'I can see she's bored, but what can I do about it? A holiday at Bodrum in summer would be better for her. She's not interested in ancient cities or beautiful scenery. She wants to dance and flirt with boys of her own age.'

Tonight the *mezes* included delicious hot courgette fritters.

When she had finished her fritters, Nuray stood up to announce, 'For our next course I've ordered a Turkish speciality called *imam bayildi*. An *imam* is the prayer leader at a mosque, and the name of this dish means "the *imam* fainted". When this dish was invented by an *imam*'s wife, it was so delicious that he fainted with pleasure. But if anyone doesn't like aubergines, there are other things you can order.'

While they were waiting for the aubergines, Nicola said, 'Serif tells me he's worked for AA since he was student. How long have you been with them, Nuray?'

'Two years. My father is very conservative. At first he didn't approve. Even in Istanbul it's still usual for Turkish girls to live with their parents until they marry.'

She was at the end of the table with Richard on her left. Turning to him, she said, 'I know that sounds old-fashioned. In London girls have more independence. I expect most of the girls in your company live away from home, don't they?'

'I would think so, yes. Does your father still disapprove?'

Tonight Nuray had on a peach-coloured shirt with the coral kerchief she had worn when he photographed her at Perge. The candlelight emphasised the length and thickness of her lashes and the lovely contour of her eyebrows. She had an irresistible smile, Nicola thought, watching her focus it on Richard.

'He's resigned to it now. Even, perhaps, a little proud of me. When I go home I have interesting things to tell him about the people I've met . . . this time a publisher. The next time I come to London, you must come and meet my sister. My brother-in-law is a surgeon. They live in South Kensington. Is that near you?'

'Not far away. I must show you what goes on in a publishing house.' He looked across the table. 'You too, Nicola, if you're interested. But perhaps you see too many books at Chatham's to want to see where they're generated.'

Before she could answer, Miles, who was next to her, said, 'Oh, you work at Chatham's, do you? I usually have a browse there if I have to go to London. An excellent shop. The staff are so splendidly knowledgeable.'

'My boss would be delighted to hear you say so.'

While Miles told her about his collection of gardening books, Nicola was aware of Nuray continuing to flirt with Richard.

Later, when they were leaving, Janet said in an undertone, 'Our guide was really turning the charm on Richard tonight, wasn't she? Perhaps she's hoping to emulate her sister and feels he's a likely candidate.'

'Perhaps,' agreed Nicola lightly.

Considering Janet's suggestion on the drive back, she didn't think it probable that Richard would fall for a Turkish girl, however attractive. Men with his background married within their own circle. The future Mrs Richard Russell would most likely come from his mother's aristocratic milieu or the equally exclusive 'old money' set in America.

The fact that, according to report, his girlfriends had been chosen for their intelligence and style didn't mean his bride would have those qualities. In Richard's social strata, good blood-stock applied to people as well as horses.

Earlier she had heard him talking to Hilary about riding holidays. Probably his performance on horseback was as impressive as the powerful crawl he had demonstrated in the sea this morning.

He was one of those fortunate people who, by a combination of natural gifts and intense application, excelled at everything they tried.

Except perhaps at close and lasting relationships. He was thirty-four and still unmarried. Why?

Because he had yet to meet the right girl? Because he preferred to remain free as long as possible? Because, in spite of his eligibility and surface charm, there were flaws, not apparent to those who knew him only slightly, which emerged on closer acquaintance?

Aware that she was spending more time thinking about him than about any of the others, Nicola made a conscious effort to turn her thoughts in other directions. Soon afterwards they arrived at the hotel.

On the top floor was a dining-room-cum-coffee-shop. Before supper, deprived of hot showers, the Tufnells had gone to some nearby shops and come back with various cakes, one of which they fetched from their room to share with the group.

Presently Richard said, 'I'm going for a stroll round town. Will anyone join me?'

When Janet, Philip and Sylvie had said they would, he turned an enquiring glance on the Tufnells.

'I'm going to finish my crossword and Joan's going to read,' said Bob.

Richard raised an interrogative eyebrow at Nicola.

She would have liked to join them, but said, 'If the water's hot now, I want to wash my hair.'

The others left but Nicola stayed talking to the Tufnells, who had ordered more coffee, for a few minutes.

In this hotel their rooms were on different floors instead of being all on one landing. Hers and Sylvie's was on the first floor.

On the second-floor landing Serif was reading a paper. As she came down the stairs from the coffee-shop, he folded it into a tight roll and stuck it in his back pocket.

'I thought you wouldn't be long. Let's go and find a bar. It's cold out...too cold for a walk.'

'I have to wash my hair.'

'You can do it in the morning. This is our only chance to be alone.'

Stepping in front of her, blocking her way down the stairs, he put his hands on her arms and drew her to him.

Instinctively Nicola's hands came up to hold him away from her. But he was too quick and too strong for her to fend him off. The next moment her hands were pressed uselessly against his chest and his mouth was on hers...

'Excuse me.'

The voice which made Serif stop kissing her was Richard's.

'Sorry to disturb you,' he said politely. 'Janet thinks she left her scarf upstairs.'

As they moved aside, he stepped past and went up the stairs in the easy three-at-a-time leaps of a long-legged man in a hurry.

He was already out of earshot when Nicola recovered herself sufficiently to say crossly, 'You're out of line, Serif.'

'Don't be cross. You'd liked it. So did I.' He attempted to draw her back to him but this time she was prepared and fended him away more vigorously.

'I *don't* like it,' she said vehemently. 'We are practically strangers. I'm not into casual kissing. I don't want a holiday romance. I mean that. I'm not playing hard to get.'

'Oh, come on...don't be like that. I thought you liked me?'

'I would...if you'd stop making passes.'

'A kiss isn't a pass,' he objected. 'Are you embarrassed because Richard saw us? So what? Unless you prefer him to me? Perhaps you want Richard to kiss you? Is that why you're angry?'

'Certainly not!'

The forceful retort was no sooner uttered than Richard came down the stairs with Janet's scarf in his hand.

'Sorry...not trying to cramp your style, Serif. But you have chosen a rather public place. Goodnight.'

For a moment, after he had brushed past them and turned the bend of the stairs to start down the next flight, he looked straight at Nicola.

What thoughts lay behind the enigmatic expression on his face it was impossible to tell.

Early the following morning, she went for a walk round the town.

She had slept badly, upset by the incident on the staircase. Annoyingly, Serif's kiss had stirred up feelings which, like a fire in a slow-burning stove flaring up when the draught-door was opened, had troubled her more last night than for a long time.

All the unsatisfied longings aroused by her holiday with Ian, and subsequently damped down, had revived. But what had kept her awake was not the possibility that in Serif's arms she might at last find the fulfilment which had eluded her in Spain.

It could be that he was a more accomplished lover than Ian. But as she was not in love with him she would never find that out.

In fact, after Richard had passed them for a second time, she had spoken to Serif in a tone which might have been so offensive to a Turkish man's pride that he wouldn't speak to her again.

Well, if he's in a huff now that's just too bad, she thought.

Serif's opinion was unimportant. It was what Richard thought that she minded.

Why?

Why should she care what he, of all people, thought? On the basis of her CV and her seniors' reports, he hadn't rated her at all highly. In fact her personal impact on him had been so slight that three years later neither her name nor her face meant a thing to him. So what did it matter that he'd caught her being kissed by Serif? Or that he must also have overheard her strenuous denial on being asked if she wanted *him* to kiss her?

The answer, which she had spent much of the night avoiding but now admitted to herself, was that she was suffering from a physical attraction so strong it amounted to infatuation.

One which was likely to prove even more abortive and painful than her previous involvement with a man.

Later that day they walked in rugged country which in past times might have sheltered brigands. Compared with English landscapes, this terrain was awesome in its wildness.

After about an hour's steady tramping, while they paused to admire a fine view, Nuray announced that in another thirty minutes they would come to a place to have tea.

'And I have some biskwits in my pack to share with you,' she added.

'What sort of biskwits?' asked Richard.

'Why are you laughing at me?' she asked, recognising, as Nicola did, the slight crinkling round his eyes and the hint of a smile at one corner of his mouth.

'The u is silent, Nuray. The English pronounce the word as if it were spelt b-i-s-k-i-t-s. In America we call them crackers.'

'Thank you for correcting me. I know I make many mistakes.'

'On the contrary, your English is very nearly perfect. I was only teasing you. In future whenever I have a "biskwit" with my tea, I'll remember you.' He put an arm round her shoulders and gave her a hug.

Had she needed confirmation of her condition, the sharp thrust of pain Nicola felt as she watched them would have told her what was the matter with her.

To the others the hug would have seemed a fraternal gesture. She suspected a deeper significance. Richard might not be falling for Nuray in any serious sense, but obviously he found her attractive. It would have been strange if he didn't. With her luxuriant black hair, flashing dark eyes and tawny skin, she *was* the most attractive woman present.

Perhaps Richard had every attention of tasting Nuray's pretty lips before the trek was over. The fact that she still lived at home, and possibly had less experience than girls of her age in western countries, might be a challenge to him.

The bar of the mountain hamlet where they stopped for tea had a beaten earth floor and open rafters. Several locals were already there, countrymen muffled against the cold in old overcoats and an assortment of other warm clothing. One had a shawl round his shoulders. Their hands were like roots, gnarled and ingrained with soil, the nails black and broken. But their faces were cheerful, their talk punctuated with chuckles and guffaws.

All the Turks were smoking. Soon Nicola found that the fug was making her eyes smart. Like Miles and Hilary, she went outside. As they were deep in conversation, she didn't join them but moved away and stood contemplating the view and sipping apple tea.

A week tomorrow some of the group would be returning to London. She had been able to book a two-day extension because, on the Monday when she should have returned to work, her boss would be in Scotland at his mother's ninetieth birthday party. As he was away that day, he had said she could take advantage of the option to extend her holiday.

'It's too smoky in there for me too.'

As Richard joined her, Nicola gave a slight jump.

'Did you ever smoke?'

She shook her head. 'My father offered a huge bribe if I stayed clear until I was nineteen. By then I had the sense to see what an expensive shackle the habit is. Have you smoked?'

'Yes... But I decided to stay with alcohol. Beer in those days. Mainly wine now. Although anyone with their ear to my wall last night would have heard the telltale glug-glug of the gin bottle. It was hellishly cold, didn't you think?'

She nodded. 'I wore my down jacket to read in bed. I couldn't get the hot-air thing to work properly.'

'They're all suffering from various degrees of burnout. This is a much poorer country than I'd realised. Like Spain in the Sixties, they need the prosperity mass tourism can bring. It will be a pity if they let all their coasts be colonised by third-rate architects designing for barbarian developers.'

'I suppose it's inevitable. Countries never seem to learn from each other's mistakes.'

Discussing the impact of tourism, Nicola relaxed. At first she had thought he intended to talk about the scene on the stairs last night; perhaps to punish her for that emphatic 'Certainly not!'.

She felt a surge of regret that they couldn't have met like this, but with the difference that she was still in publishing but had never worked for Barking & Dollis. They would have had so much in common, so many things to talk about.

'There seems to be something about you the Turks find irresistible.'

Both the statement and the sudden change in Richard's tone and expression made her realise she had relaxed too soon. 'It could make your life complicated if you were here on your own.'

Refusing to be drawn, she said, 'You're really working on your Turkish. The old men in there were delighted to find a foreigner speaking some of their language.'

'I'm trying, but you know what they say about languages.'

'No?'

'The best place to pick them up fast is in bed. I'm sure Serif would be pleased to give you some private tuition.'

'Perhaps, but I'm not interested.'

'In improving your Turkish...or in Serif?'

'I have as much Turkish as I need, and brief encounters aren't my style.'

Janet came out of the bar and strolled over to join them. 'I'm getting a sore throat in there. I hear we're having fresh trout for dinner...at that place where we left the truck. I feel sorry for Lorna, being stuck there for four hours,' she added.

Lorna had opted out of the afternoon walk.

'She has Serif with her,' said Richard. 'He's good company, isn't he, Nicola?'

She could tell that he didn't believe her claim to be indifferent to the Turk. If only he knew who really had the power to turn her on. But that, thank God, was something he would never suspect if she could help it.

'It looks as if we're on the move,' he said. 'Shall I take your glass back for you?'

As the empty tea-glass changed hands, their fingers were in fleeting contact. Her reaction to his touch was a mixture of pleasure and despair. How could this have happened to her so quickly?

On the return walk she came to the conclusion that any holiday of this kind must act as a forcing house for all human relationships. Mainly it was friendship which flourished more quickly than in normal conditions. Possibly, sometimes, animosities sprouted. But who would have thought that, not quite a week after seeing him at Heathrow, her feelings about Richard Russell would have changed so dramatically? From intense dislike to unwilling attraction in six days. It didn't seem possible, but it was so.

'This time last week we were packing to come away,' said Janet. 'This time next week we'll be on the train back to Istanbul.'

Nicola knew that the next seven days would be a bitter-sweet time which her head would want to pass as quickly as possible, while her foolish infatuated senses would treasure every hour, dreading the end of the journey.

By half-past ten the next day they were hurtling along the coast on a road blasted out of undulating red cliffs rising from the sea. The water lapping the many small empty beaches tucked in the curves of the cliffs looked invitingly clear.

Serif was in high spirits. The rock and roll tape he was playing was being relayed to the trekkers. Through the rear window of the cab they could see him beating time on the steering-wheel.

Every few minutes he took a bend perilously close to the edge of the tarred surface and a twenty-foot drop into the sea.

Nicola was sitting on the offside of the vehicle, leaning forward to peer at a cluster of holiday villas under construction on the clifftop, when the truck swung sideways to avoid an oncoming lorry. The movement sent loose objects flying, made Joan give a cry of alarm and pitched Nicola across the aisle.

She was fielded by Richard, sitting opposite. He grabbed her by both upper arms and for a few seconds his fingers felt like steel clamps.

'I'm sorry,' she said, as he rose from his seat and lifted her back into hers.

'No problem.' He let her go and bent to retrieve a book which had fallen from the seat beside hers.

Before resuming his place he moved to the front of the truck, holding the overhead rail, and switched off the relay outlet, silencing Serif's choice of music.

'You mean thing! I like that tape,' Sylvie objected.

'You may, but the grown-ups don't.'

He smiled as he said it. Nicola, watching, saw Sylvie pull a face, in much the same way that Nicola, in her teens, had sometimes reacted to being told off by her brother.

'Would you like to borrow my head-set, Sylvie?' she offered.

'What sort of music is it? I don't go for classical stuff.'

'It's a mixture. Give it a trial for ten minutes. You might like some of it.'

'OK.'

About mid-morning they stopped on the outskirts of Kale where, in an open space, a large number of people were assembling.

After Serif had leaned from his window to speak to some bystanders, Nuray came back to tell the group what was happening.

'There's a market here today and also, soon, *deve güresi* . . . camel fighting.'

'I certainly don't wish to see *that*,' Hilary said firmly. 'The market—yes. But animals being made to fight is not my idea of entertainment.'

Most people murmured agreement. Nuray said, 'OK, we'll look round the market and then drive through the town to see the rock tombs in the cliffs.'

Many of the market stalls were festooned with lengths of fabric for the traditional baggy trousers called *samlar* worn by the women. There were also stands selling track suits, trainers and the cheap plastic toys to be found in markets worldwide.

'Serif seems to take the view that women don't mind a little forceful persuasion.'

Nicola looked up to find Richard beside her. No one else from the group was near by. She replaced the string of beads she had been looking at. 'He would lose his job if he barged into our bedrooms. Anyway, why should he need to? I'm sure he has girlfriends galore. There's probably one of them waiting for him at Kas.'

'It was you he was kissing at Finike the night before last.'

'He was just trying it on. Men do. Haven't you... in the past?'

'I'm thirty-four, Nicola, not sixty-four. My wild oats aren't that far behind me.'

'I know that,' she said unguardedly. 'They're still being sown, so one hears.'

'They are? It's news to me. Where did you pick that up?'

'I don't remember.'

'I think you do,' he said shrewdly. As she moved on to the next stall, his hand fell on her shoulder, lightly but making it clear she was not going to get away until she had provided a more satisfactory answer to his question.

'I probably read something about you in one of the trade papers. My boss leaves them lying around and I sometimes look through them in my lunch break.'

'I read them too and I don't recall any references to my personal life.'

'Perhaps it wasn't a direct reference to you. It may have been in that column where the writer makes oblique digs at the well-known people in publishing. Perhaps it was someone else at Barking & Dollis he called a Casanova.'

'It must have been,' he said drily, removing his hand from her shoulder. 'It certainly wasn't me.'

A small Turkish child standing on a box behind the next stall gave them a big smile. 'Hello.'

'Hello.' Richard leaned his tall frame over the wares on display to ruffle the child's curly head.

Other children, playing in the space between the two lines of stalls, ran up to demonstrate that they too knew foreign greetings.

'Hello. *Bonjour, monsieur. Guten tag.*'

'Do you like children, Nicola?' he asked.

'I haven't had much to do with them. My brother isn't married yet. Both my parents were only children, so we don't have any cousins.'

'I have seven small nephews and nieces and a lot of my friends have children, except those whose wives have careers and are putting it off.' His tone was neutral, giving no clue to where he stood on that issue. 'I already have four godchildren. So that's eleven birthdays to be remembered. Fortunately my computer warns me ahead of time.'

'Perhaps you'll be able to stock up with presents at the Grand Bazaar next Saturday.'

'Maybe, although Nuray says a better place to shop is a newly built mall in the suburbs. Tell me, was it because you were under a misapprehension about my attitude to women that you were noticeably stand-offish at the beginning of the trip?'

She had thought they were back on safe ground and was disconcerted.

'I was? Perhaps you imagined it.'

'I don't think I did. If I'm wrong, why didn't you tell me you knew who I was? It would have been the natural thing to do—if you hadn't already decided to dislike me.'

He was right, of course. Had he been at the helm or on the staff of any other publishing company, she *would* have made friendly overtures. She would probably have mentioned her connection with Barking & Dollis.

In the publishing trade as a whole, there had been a great deal of sympathy for the victims of the purges. Some—mainly people more senior than herself—had been taken on by rival companies, one or two actually being promoted to better positions than the jobs they had lost.

She decided the only way to deal with this interrogation was to turn it around and throw a question at him.

'Did it bother you?'

# CHAPTER EIGHT

'NATURALLY. Any normal person is bothered by a hostile reaction . . . especially from someone they don't know.' After a pause, Richard added, 'And particularly from someone they'd like to know better.'

His tone made Nicola's heart flip. Was she reading more into the statement than he intended? Probably he was only referring to the connection between publishing and bookselling.

In her most casual tone, she said, 'Now we *all* know each other better. Considering the diversity of our ages, backgrounds and everything, we've homogenised well, haven't we? That's probably one of the best things about this type of holiday—the opportunity to get to know people one would never normally meet.'

'And, in some cases, wouldn't want to,' was Richard's sardonic comment.

On the way back to the truck, the trekkers couldn't avoid seeing two of the camels fighting.

But it wasn't the gory battle Nicola and Hilary had envisaged. In fact the bout in progress as they passed was rather less violent than two women elbowing each other in a scrimmage for sale bargains. Held by their owners, the camels lurched sideways at each other. Both were frothing at the mouth.

'But because their bits are uncomfortable, I should think, rather than because their blood is up,' said Hilary.

Standing or squatting in a wide circle around the beasts engaged in desultory combat were two or three hundred Turks, the female spectators segregated on a bank of gravel forming a convenient grandstand.

When Stuart paused to photograph one of the hobbled animals, its owner came rushing up to demand a fee.

Stuart was annoyed. 'To hell with that,' he said crossly.

Richard laughed. 'Come on, Stuart. Give the guy a thousand *lira*. You'd pay that for a postcard.'

'That's different. This is a rip-off.'

'OK, it's a rip-off. But you have to give him marks for trying. I expect he has a lot of mouths to feed.'

'Not at my expense.' Stuart stalked off.

Richard shrugged and exchanged looks with Hilary. Watching them walking ahead of her, Nicola envied their easy companionship.

On the other side of town, with the group gathered round her, Nuray said, 'These Lycian rock tombs you can see in the cliffs behind me are among the most beautiful and interesting antiquities in Turkey. In summer this place would be swarming with visitors. Today we are the only people here. Before you explore the Greco-Roman theatre and climb up to the tombs, let's refresh ourselves with orange juice.'

As the orange-juice seller had only a hand-press and it was going to take some time to make juice for everyone, Nicola thought she would explore first and have a drink later.

Presently, trying to find her way towards the tombs without going back to the main entrance to the theatre, she came to a place where the stone ledge on which she was standing was about four feet above the grassy path below.

It was too far to jump. Before she could sit on the edge and lower herself down, Serif appeared.

'Do you want to come down? I'll help you.' He held out his arms to her.

It was difficult to refuse without seeming rude. Reluctantly she put her hands on his shoulders and let him swing her off the ledge. Then, instead of letting her go, he kept his hands on her waist.

'Are you still angry because I kissed you?'

There were people near by. She could hear several voices.

'No, but please let me go.'

Instead his hold on her tightened. As she turned her face sideways, trying to elude his mouth, he slid one arm further round her, using the other hand to turn her face towards him. He wasn't rough, but he was strong, and determined their lips were going to meet. Short of methods the situation didn't justify, there was nothing she could do to stop him.

Knowing from the sound of the voices that they weren't going to be alone for much longer, Nicola gave in and let him kiss her.

'Ooh, I say! What's going on here?'

Mrs Tufnell's voice behind him—half excited, half shocked—made Serif raise his head.

'Oh, it's you two,' Joan said, as he and Nicola moved apart. 'I didn't recognise you for a minute.'

With her were Philip and Bob.

'It's a bit early in the day for that sort of thing, isn't it, lad?' her husband remarked, in a jocular tone. 'Still, you're only young once.' He gave Nicola a wink. 'And it's not a proper holiday without a dash of romance, is it?'

Later, on the way to the next night stop, they spent half an hour playing energetic beach football.

Richard scored his goals with an amused shrug, not the jubilant clasping of hands over heads which were Serif's and Stuart's reactions when they kicked the ball into the improvised goals ineffectively defended by Philip at one end of the pitch and by Bob at the other.

'You lot look like lobsters. Joan and I are freezing,' said Janet, when the others returned to the truck. 'It's high time the heater was mended. Serif should have fixed it this morning instead of chasing Nicola around the ruins.'

Richard heard the remark and raised an eyebrow.

'Chasing you, Nicola?'

'Janet's exaggerating.'

At this point, as she had earlier, Hilary smoothed over what, from Nicola's point of view, was Janet's gaffe.

'Perhaps the heater can be attended to while we're at Kas. Why don't you and Miles have a word with Serif this evening, Richard? It certainly ought to be mended before we go back over the mountains.'

'We'll do that,' said Richard. 'Serif does seem to be letting his duties as driver-mechanic take second place to his social activities,' he added, with an enigmatic glance at Nicola.

She had thought Serif attractive when they had met and, in his audacious black-eyed way, he was. But the way she felt now about Richard made her impervious to the Turk's charisma. He had become a complication and a nuisance. Even the way he played football seemed to her too flamboyant compared with the more relaxed style of the tall American.

Before they arrived at the next place on the itinerary, Serif stopped the truck for Nuray to join the group.

'In Turkish, K-a-s is pronounced like your word cash,' she told them. 'Kas is the site of the ancient city of Antiphellos and we know that in Roman times it was famous for its sponges. A few years ago it was a fishing port. Now it caters to many tourists, but not at this time of year.'

The Oteli Ekici, their base for the next two nights, was a newly built hotel. With its rows of small balconies, it resembled the thousands of hotels constructed to house package-tourists in resorts all round the Mediterranean. Its only distinguishing feature was a lobby floor spread with colourful rugs.

Here, to their mutual pleasure, Nicola and Hilary were assigned to the same room.

'Janet is neat and considerate, but I don't find her as compatible,' said Hilary, as they unpacked their belongings.

Although the radiators weren't on, the water in the bathroom was hot and they both had a shower and washed out their smalls, pegging them out on a rack provided for that purpose on the minuscule balcony.

Their room overlooked a colony of similar hotels, all the others closed up for the winter. However, on leaving the hotel they discovered that, in the opposite direction, lay an attractive harbour and beside it a triangular space with some trees and a statue of Kemal Atutürk, the founder of modern Turkey.

While they were exploring, they met Richard, who was looking for a bottle of Turkish brandy, and found a small bottles of cheap *kanyak* in a shop near the vegetable market. From there the three of them wandered around, discovering a cobbled street of attractive old timber houses with a beautiful Lycian tomb at the top of it.

'How about a pre-dinner drink in my room?' said Richard, when they returned to the hotel.

Later, when they were tidying themselves for supper, Hilary said, 'He's rather an enigma, isn't he? Far more at ease than Philip, far more outgoing than Miles, and yet I sense a reserve ... a part of himself he holds back. What do you think about him, Nicola?'

'I don't know. He's out of my league. I'm not used to hobnobbing with chief executives.'

'Most people haven't reached those heights at Richard's age. He must be exceptionally clever.'

There had been a time, immediately after her dismissal, when Nicola had felt that nepotism had a good deal to do with Richard's early eminence. Since then she had changed that view. There could be no doubt that his incisive leadership had saved Barking & Dollis from disaster.

His innovative ideas and the reforms he had instituted were the talk of the trade. This year the firm was expected to win the coveted Publisher of the Year award. Considering how recently it had been in the doldrums, to receive that accolade would be a remarkable achievement.

'I've heard people in the book trade speak highly of him,' she said, in a neutral tone.

She knew Hilary was very perceptive and didn't want her to guess how she felt about Richard. She valued Hilary's opinion of her and felt sure the older woman would think it foolish to succumb to an attraction so quickly. And she would be right.

They had dinner at a small restaurant on the waterfront. The meal started with *sigara boregi*, hot, crisp 'cigarettes' of fine pastry filled with cheese. These were followed by spinach in a savoury gravy and then by grilled meat with mushrooms.

When everyone had finished the main course, Nuray said, 'I suggest we leave here now and go to a place near the post office where they serve cakes and hot chocolate.'

It was on the way to the cake bar that Sylvie tripped and fell over. She picked herself up, unhurt except for her hand which was badly grazed.

'I'll come back to the hotel and dress it for you,' said Nicola. As it was Sylvie's right hand, she wouldn't be able to deal with the injury herself. 'Explain to the others what's happened, will you, Hilary?'

The group had left the restaurant together but some had walked faster than others and the three of them had stopped to look in the window of a shop selling china.

At the hotel it emerged that Sylvie had come away without even a sticking plaster in her baggage. Fortunately Nicola had a basic first-aid kit, so they went to her room.

By the time they got there, the clean tissues she had given Sylvie to stop blood dripping on her clothes were soaked.

Sylvie had tripped on a chunk of breeze block half hidden in a mound of grit by a building site. When she saw how much grit was embedded in the heel of her hand, she paled, her eyes brimming with tears.

'Don't watch if it makes you feel queasy,' Nicola advised.

Cleaning the wound was going to be painful. She wished the group included someone more expert than herself.

Sylvie was crying, and Nicola was trying to be both gentle and quick, when there was a knock at the door.

Wondering if the desk clerk who had given them their keys, and seen the bloody tissues wrapping Sylvie's hand, could have sent for a doctor, Nicola left the younger girl perched on the lid of the lavatory while she opened the door.

'I thought you might need help,' said Richard. He was carrying a plastic box and a mini immersion heater.

'I'm trying to get all the grit out of Sylvie's hand. It's a bit tricky.'

The bathroom wasn't large. With Richard there it seemed even smaller. But his presence put a brake on Sylvie's tears and cries of pain.

'You need a cup of tea. Nicola will make it while I finish doing your hand,' he said, taking charge.

Nicola was only too willing to relinquish control. As she carried out his instruction to make tea, she realised that as soon as she saw him standing outside she had felt a wave of relief. It wasn't that she was unequal to coping with a minor emergency if she had to, but she knew Richard would be better at subjecting Sylvie to pain now to prevent infection later.

Presently she emerged, her hand neatly bandaged.

'Richard's cleaning the basin.'

'Sit down and drink this.' Nicola put a mug of tea into her good hand. 'If I were you, I'd go to bed. It's cold out and you've had a shock.'

Richard emerged from the bathroom.

'Are you up to date with your shots, Sylvie?'

She looked blank until Nicola asked, 'When did you last have a tetanus booster?'

'Oh...not long ago.' Sylvie put aside the mug. 'I'm all right now. Let's go back to the others.'

Richard shook his head. 'You're going to bed. Doctor's orders.'

'I'm not going to stay behind while everybody else has fun.'

'I doubt if you're missing anything wonderful and we're staying too, aren't we, Nicola? We're going down to the bar, and you're going to swallow this pill and get a good night's rest. It's a big day tomorrow...the boat trip.'

Nicola felt sure that if she had prescribed an early night Sylvie would have rebelled. When Richard laid down the law, she grumbled but obeyed.

On their way downstairs, he said, 'It was good of you to come back with her. When Hilary told us what had happened, I thought I'd follow in case Sylvie was giving you trouble. She's not the type to bite the bullet.'

'I was very glad to see you,' Nicola admitted.

'Good...we're making headway.' The remark, and the tone in which he said it, made her pulses quicken.

The hotel did not have a bar as such. Drinks were served at the sofas in the reception-cum-television lounge. The desk clerk was watching a programme but responded to Richard's request for coffee with cheerful alacrity.

'While he's out of the way, let's turn the volume down,' said Richard.

He succeeded in reducing the noise level but, even though they chose a sofa with a pillar between it and the TV, the sound of a Turkish game show was still intrusive.

When the clerk returned with their tray, Richard said, 'Let's take it up to the first-floor landing. I noticed a sofa there and we shan't have to compete with the noise from the box.'

The sofa he meant was at the junction of two long corridors, facing the door of the lift.

'Not where I should choose to have coffee, but it seems to be our only option,' said Richard. There being no table, he put the tray down on the middle of the sofa's three squabs.

'And we can intercept Sylvie if she tries to sneak out in the hope of seeing that Tasmanian boy who was chatting her up in the restaurant,' said Nicola. 'Although I don't think she will. She's quite in awe of you.'

'You can't blame her for wanting more action than the trip offers anyone of her age. But before we leave Kas, so Nuray tells me, we're going to eat at the town's smartest dine-and-dance place.' He poured out the coffee. 'I suspect it's the only one open at this time of year. In summer the harbour will be full of private and charter yachts. Instead of sitting up here, we'd be at a table on the waterfront, watching the world go by.'

He handed her a cup. As he picked up the other, he said, '*Mutluluga*...to happiness.'

'*Mutluluga*,' she echoed, knowing she would rather be here, in the dimly lit and unheated corridor of an almost empty hotel with this man, than in the most glamorous place in the world with another man.

The only thing better would be to be in Richard's room, in his bed, in his arms.

Was that his objective? she wondered. Was he, like Sylvie, impatient to see more action than the holiday had offered so far? Had he decided that, of the three available women, she would be the least trouble, not only to get into bed but also to drop when the trek ended?

Being the first down to breakfast, Nicola chose a chair facing the sea and sat thinking about last night.

Was she glad or sorry Richard hadn't made a pass at her? It was one of those questions to which there was no cut-and-dried answer.

Her feelings about the way the evening had ended were a mixture of relief, disappointment, pique, puzzlement and unsatisfied longing. She wanted Richard more than she had ever wanted Ian. And, last night, desire might have proved stronger than discretion had Richard tried to coax her to spend the night with him.

But perhaps he had remembered what she had temporarily forgotten: that what he did at night was his own affair, but *her* absence from her room would be noticed and might even cause some alarm if Hilary failed to grasp the reason for it.

Whatever his reason for *not* making a pass—the most obvious one being that he wasn't sufficiently attracted to her—he had seemed to find her company enjoyable. They had talked until Hilary had stepped out of the lift, having left the others still talking at the cake bar.

After a short conversation, Hilary had taken the room-key and five minutes later Nicola had said goodnight to Richard and followed her.

There was snow on the tops of the foothills through which they drove to reach the village of Üçagiz where a boat would be waiting to take them to Kekova Island.

Üçagiz had only recently been connected to the coastal road system. Before that, access had been by boat and rough track, which had kept the village from being spoilt. Now its long seclusion was ending and, because of its picturesque situation, it was in danger of being ruined. Nuray said they might be among the last people to see it untarnished by tourism.

In an open square in the centre of Üçagiz—which Nuray said was pronounced Uchaz—several girls and two older women were awaiting the arrival of the bus with shallow baskets filled with cotton scarves similar to the ones on their own heads.

It was a short walk to the jetty where a fisherman, whom Nuray called Uncle Arif—uncle being a courtesy

title—kept his boat. The small foredeck was spread with
a rug and the seats along the sides with Turkish runners.

Soon everyone was aboard, the engine was throbbing
and they were moving away from the wharf and beginning to see Üçagiz in its entirety, a huddle of small,
red-roofed houses against a backcloth of arid hills and
blue sky, the dominant feature being a white minaret
topped by an emerald-green spire.

'We're going to a place where you can bathe,' said
Nuray, as the boat neared a rocky cove.

Nicola leaned over the side and dabbled her hand in
the water. It felt cold but was clear as stained glass, the
pebbles on the bed as distinct as if they were inches rather
than feet below the surface.

With the boat moored to a convenient rock, the passengers scrambled ashore. There were plenty of places
where those who wanted to swim could undress.

The sun felt gloriously warm on Nicola's bare back
as she stood on one leg to buckle a plastic sandal on the
other foot.

Richard and Miles were already in the sea when she
plunged in, stifling a shriek as the cold water embraced
her. But it wasn't long before her body adjusted. After
some energetic swimming all the bathers came out feeling
invigorated and chiding the others for missing a great
experience.

'Nicola...are you decent?'

Miles's voice brought her out from behind the rock
where she had been changing to find him offering her a
biscuit.

'Oh, lovely...digestives...my favourites. Thanks,
Miles.'

'Richard's dispensing brandy, if you fancy a tot.'

'Why not? Although I'm not cold now...gloriously
warm.'

They made their way to where Richard was pouring
out *kanyak*.

He had replaced his wet shorts with a towel wrapped round his lean hips. In the bright morning light, his skin had a burnished sheen which made her long to run her fingers over the powerful contours of his shoulders and chest.

She found it difficult to keep her eyes off him. It seemed almost unfair that, with all his other advantages, he should also be good to look at. But she mustn't allow herself to watch him. If she did, it would soon be noticed, and she couldn't bear anyone to guess that she found him wildly attractive.

Back in the boat, they were taken to see an island which had been the site of a long-submerged city. Its quay and other ruined buildings were still visible in the clear water. But according to Miles and Hilary the most memorable feature of the place was the vivid green euphorbia bushes growing above the drowned city to a much greater size than either of the group's two keen gardeners had ever seen before.

Simena, where they were to lunch, was built on the side of a hill crowned by the crumbling walls of a large castle.

As she stepped ashore, Nicola noticed a beautifully carved stone capital standing upside-down on the quay, topped by a plant in a can which had once held paint for the boats pulled up on the nearby hard.

They ate out of doors on a terrace which in summer would be shaded by cane blinds spread across the rafters overhead.

Cane-shaded light bulbs wired to the rafters indicated that, later in the year, meals were also served here after dark. It was easy to imagine the sea gleaming in the moonlight, the black silhouettes of the islands, and the coloured riding lights of visiting yachts moored down in the harbour.

Nicola found herself thinking what a lovely place it would be for a seagoing honeymoon. Angry with herself for indulging in wishful thinking, she passed the empty chair next to Richard and sat next to Miles.

# CHAPTER NINE

THE following afternoon they were taken to see a display of handmade carpets. The shop's owner, said Nuray, would also explain how the rugs were made and what the patterns signified.

The seating consisted of two narrow stone benches built along right-angled walls which, hung with rugs, served as backrests. Nicola found herself squeezed between Richard and Bob.

The display began with the service of apple tea, after which the young bearded dealer, speaking excellent English, began to unfold the neat stacks of flat-weave kilims and hand-knotted pile rugs, some new, some antique.

He had the enthusiasm of a man with a deep knowledge and love of the wares he sold. Very soon the floor of the shop was piled knee-high with a profusion of rich colours and fanciful patterns.

'Are you going to buy one?' Nicola murmured, while a second tray of tea was being served.

Bob thought she was speaking to him. 'That depends what he's asking. Joan'll know if they're reasonable. A very keen shopper is my wife.'

Nicola glanced enquiringly at Richard. To take up a minimum of space, he was sitting with his shoulders pulled forward as much as possible and his hands clipped between his long thighs.

'I think so. What about you?'

She shook her head. 'I'd like to but can't afford it...even if they are bargains. All my resources are already earmarked.'

She wondered what he would say if he knew about The Project. He would probably tell her she and Gina were mad.

The rug in which Richard was interested was the one Nicola would have chosen had money been no object. It was an intricate design of many strange birds and animals worked in sophisticated colours on a ground of off-white silk. Intended to cover a wall rather than a floor, not surprisingly it was more expensive than the rugs already priced.

Had she not been committed to The Project, she would have enjoyed buying a rug as a present for her parents. But she and Gina had agreed to cut out all self-indulgence in order to minimise the amount they were borrowing from their banks. Nicola wouldn't have been here but for Aunt Ruth's generosity. But now, ten days away from wintry London, breathing an unpolluted mixture of mountain and sea air, eating well, walking a lot, swimming, she was feeling very much peppier than when she had set out.

Outside the shop, Hilary said, 'Nuray, are those firm prices he gave us? Or are we meant to bargain?'

'They're good prices; better, I believe, than you'll find in Istanbul. And he's a reputable dealer who supplies several of the best specialist rug shops in London. If you want the rug mailed to you, you can rely on its arrival.'

Standing behind her, Serif said, 'Turkish rugs are a very good souvenir of your holiday. Better than Turkish delight…"a moment on the lips, a lifetime on the hips".'

'Where did you learn that expression?' Joan asked.

'From an American lady.'

'I'm going for a walk round the block, Nicola, and then I shall look at "my" rug again,' said Hilary. 'I'll see you later.'

As the group dispersed, Serif fell into step with Nicola who was heading uphill. 'You didn't see anything you liked?

'Several I liked very much. But I haven't the money to buy one.'

'You don't need money. You can pay with your credit card.'

'A card isn't a magic wand, Serif. I'd have to find the cash later.'

That seemed to puzzle him. 'If you were poor, you wouldn't be here,' he said. 'This holiday isn't expensive, but for what it costs you in England many people in Turkey could live for a long time.'

'I'm not poor. But I don't need a rug and the money I earn is being put by for something else.'

'A car?' he asked.

'No, not a car. I don't need one.'

'I'd like a Mercedes sports model . . . a beautiful car,' he said, half closing his eyes. Then, looking sideways at her, 'Would you like me better if I had a Mercedes?'

'Possibly a lot less. An expensive car might make you insufferably pleased with yourself. You don't suffer from an inferiority complex as things are,' she added, laughing.

'My word, I wouldn't have recognised you,' said Hilary, when she came up to change for the evening and found Nicola ready to go down. 'You look quite different with your hair up and all that make-up.'

'Too much make-up, do you think?' Nicola had borrowed some from Sylvie.

Hilary studied her for a moment. 'No, probably not. Certainly no more than most young things wear at parties, and Janet puts on all the time. I'm just not used to seeing it on you.'

Nicola gave herself a final inspection in the dressing-table mirror. She had put up her hair with a pair of tortoiseshell clips and was wearing a pair of flamboyant silver and gilt earrings Peter had brought back from a visit to Java. Her silk T-shirt was grey, the same colour as her eyes. Tonight she had on her best jeans and, in-

stead of the braided leather belt usually slotted through
the loops on the waistband, she had pulled through a
long Indian scarf in grey and two shades of blue.

There was no one in the reception lounge when she
went downstairs. She sat on one of the sofas, feeling
increasingly jittery as the moment when Richard might
finally recognise her approached.

Although her hairstyle tonight was not the same as
the cut she had had the day he'd sacked her, it was closer
to that style than the casual ponytail she had worn since
the trek started. And the make-up and earrings must
make her look more like the Nicola Temple he had met
three years ago.

Usually he was one of the first to appear whenever
the group assembled. Would he be early tonight?

To relax the tight knot of tension inside her, she made
herself take some deep breaths. Anyone would think she
was waiting for an important interview on which her
future depended.

When Richard came down the stairs, she saw him before
he saw her, half hidden by one of the large columns between the foot of the staircase and the corner where she
was sitting.

He was dressed in a low-key style with grey trousers
and a grey sweater, with a striped shirt showing at the
V-neck and his anorak over his arm.

As she rose and stepped into view, he stopped short
on his way to desk.

'Nicola!' he exclaimed, in an odd tone. As he took in
her upswept hair, made-up face and silk top, his eyebrows rose. 'You're a knockout!'

'Thank you.'

'This is your London persona, I take it?'

She nodded. 'Hilary claimed not to recognise me. Does
a little more make-up really make so much difference?'

He gave her a long, intent look. She waited, holding her breath, for the penny to drop. If it did, how would he handle the situation?

But what he finally said was, 'No, not really. You remind me of a line in one of my favourite books. I doubt if you would have read it. It's an American biography of a man called Maxwell Perkins. He was an editor for Scribner's, one of the great US publishing houses. It was Perkins who discovered and nurtured Ernest Hemingway and F. Scott Fitzgerald and other famous writers of the inter-war period.'

Nicola had read the book many times. Maxwell Perkins was one of her heroes, as much for his qualities as a man as for his place at the head of her former profession. But she didn't tell Richard she knew the book almost by heart.

'What's the line I remind you of?'

'It's a quotation from Virgil. *Dea incessu patuit*. But I won't tell you what it means. Read the book when you get back to London. I'm sure Chatham's will have it.'

The lift door opened and Lorna and Stuart stepped out, followed by Philip. Otherwise Nicola's face might have shown she already knew what the words meant and was thrown completely off balance by them.

Lorna was wearing a clinging black body and black tights with a short tiger-striped lamé wrap-around skirt.

'All ready for our rave-up?' she asked brightly. Then, giving Stuart a nudge, 'What about a drink while we're waiting for the others to come down?'

It wasn't until later, when they were walking to the restaurant, that Nicola had a chance to think about what Richard had said to her earlier.

The Latin phrase he had quoted came from a part of the biography which dealt with Maxwell Perkins' first meeting with the woman most people thought to have been the love of his life.

In a note to her, he had written, 'I always greatly liked the phrase "*dea incessu patuit*". But I never really knew its meaning till I saw you coming toward me through our hall the other night.'

Translated, the words meant 'she revealed herself to be a goddess'.

Could Richard really have meant that he thought *she* looked like a goddess? Nicola wondered disbelievingly. Yet what other construction was there to put on his statement?

A log fire was adding its cheerful blaze to the glow of a line of candles on the long table prepared for them at a restaurant overlooking the harbour. Turkish music was playing. An appetising aroma was wafting from the kitchen. All the staff seemed pleased to see them, hurrying to help with coats, pull out chairs and take orders for drinks. It was the most welcoming place they had been to so far.

Or was her impression coloured by the astounding compliment she had received? Nicola asked herself as she sat down. A compliment she wasn't supposed to have understood.

Whether by chance or contrivance Richard took the chair next to hers. They were both on the outer side of the table, the people opposite having their backs to a wall.

When everyone was seated, Nuray tapped a glass with a spoon. As the chatter of voices muted, she said, 'Tonight, as a special treat, we're going to have *kalamar* for our main course. But the food isn't ready yet, so why don't we all dance?'

Whereupon she and Serif moved into the space between the tables and began dancing together in a style which combined western disco with spasms of vigorous belly-dance shoulder-shaking and hip-grinding.

The party went on till late, a few locals coming in to eat, or to drink at the bar, and the staff joining in the dancing after the kitchen had closed.

The first to leave were the Tufnells, followed a little later by Miles, Hilary and Janet. Nicola didn't notice Stuart and Lorna leaving, or Philip. Suddenly it was midnight and the only people left from the group were Serif and Nuray, herself and Richard, and Sylvie who was being partnered by a young member of the staff.

'I think I'll call it a night.' Nicola got down from her stool at the bar where, at Serif's insistence, she had been trying some *raki*.

'I'll come with you,' said Richard, draining his glass.

After the noise and the warmth of the restaurant, it seemed very cold and quiet in the street outside. In spite of her padded jacket, she shivered and stepped out briskly.

'It was a good evening, didn't you think?' she said.

'Yes . . . a lot of fun.'

'I'd love to have a video of Hilary dancing with Serif.'

'She's a good sport,' Richard agreed.

He sounded slightly abstracted, making her wonder if really the evening had bored him. It had not, by sophisticated standards, been anything remarkable. And, even if he was not a regular nightclubber, he must in his time have been to all the best places in New York, London and many other cities with famous nightspots.

They walked up the hill in silence. There were not many lights on now. In summer the people of Kas stayed up late in the service of the new tourist industry. But at this time of year they reverted to traditional habits. Probably in the whole town not more than a dozen people were still awake.

At the corner where the road went in four directions, a tree made a patch of black shadow. As they reached it, Richard took her lightly but firmly by the shoulders and swung her against him.

'This is what I've been waiting for.'

He kissed her.

*   *   *

'Where do we go from here?' he murmured, a little while later, his lips against her cheek.

Nicola, who was feeling as if she had drunk several glasses of *raki* in rapid succession, made an effort to sound clear-headed.

'To bed,' she said firmly, pushing against his chest.

He loosened his hold on her slightly but kept her in the circle of his arms. 'That's fine by me. As long as you don't mind Hilary knowing about us?'

She pushed him away more vigorously. 'That's not what I meant at all!'

'It wasn't?' There was laughter in his voice. 'Well, maybe you're right. We'll be back in Istanbul soon, and meanwhile I can at least kiss you.'

He kissed her again, this time with even more assurance.

There had been nothing tentative about his first kiss. He had known she would respond, and she had. Now, as he kissed her for the second time, she knew it would be futile to pretend she didn't want him. All she could do was hope he would never discover the real reason for her rapid response.

She would rather be taken for an easy conquest than have him guess the truth: that she was helplessly infatuated.

The desk clerk was watching a chorus line of scantily clad girls on TV when they entered the hotel. He gave Richard his key and went back to his seat as they turned towards the stairs.

As they reached the landing, Nicola wondered if he would try to coax her to end the evening in his room. Probably Hilary was asleep by now. There was really nothing to stop her staying out as long as she pleased . . . until five o'clock in the morning, if she felt like it.

Halfway along the corridor, where the bedrooms were unoccupied and no one would be disturbed by the murmur of voices, he said in a low tone, 'If we must say goodnight, we'd better do it here.'

After he had kissed her in the street, the shadow of the tree had masked the expression on his face. But even here, close to a wall light, she found it impossible to guess the thoughts in his mind as he looked down at her.

Was this, on his side, merely a physical attraction? Or something more?

Richard took her face between his palms and moved them lightly over her cheeks for a moment. Then his fingers slid to the back of her head and she felt him unfastening her hair.

He must have done it before, with other women. When he had taken off the clips he felt for the pins, putting them into the pocket of her jacket before spreading her hair over her shoulders.

'You don't look much older than Sylvie with your hair down. Maybe it's just as well you do have a chaperon.'

'Maybe it is.' She slipped both arms round his neck, drew his head down and gave him a warm kiss.

But when he would have prolonged it, she broke away and said firmly, 'Goodnight, Richard. See you tomorrow.'

He had already eaten his breakfast when Nicola and Hilary arrived in the dining-room next morning. By the time they had made their selections from the buffet, he was leaving the room.

'Good morning. I'm going to the bank to cash some traveller's cheques,' he told them.

The remark was addressed to them both and there was nothing in the smiling glance he gave Nicola to distinguish it from the way he looked at Hilary. When he had gone and she was starting her breakfast, she could almost believe she had dreamed last night's kisses.

Conversation at the table was mainly about how much money would be needed for the remainder of the trip. Nicola's preoccupation wasn't whether she was going to need more Turkish *lira*, but what Richard had had in mind when, last night, he had said, 'We'll be back in Istanbul soon...'

Was he going to suggest they spend the final nights of the trip together, away from the others? Was she going to fall in with that plan? Was it his intention to see more of her after they returned to London? Or was it strictly a holiday affair which would end when they parted company in the baggage hall at Heathrow?

Somehow, between now and Thursday evening, when they would be catching the train back to the city, she had to make up her mind exactly where she stood and what she intended to do.

Lunch was a picnic eaten among the ruins of the hilltop city of Xanthus, looking down at a river from a height of several hundred feet.

They ended the day at Fethiye, a yachting centre and the last place they were to stay before heading back towards Istanbul.

On their last night on the coast, Nicola went to bed in a quandary. Had Richard's kisses at Kas, the night before last, been merely an impulse he had since regretted and didn't intend to repeat?

Neither last night nor today had he made any noticeable effort to spend time alone with her.

That night the temperature dropped. They woke up to a cold, wintry morning. The breakfast waiter was wearing a woolly ski cap with a scarf wrapped round the lower part of his face when Nicola and Hilary went up to the top-floor restaurant for breakfast. His response to their smiling, '*Günaydin*,' was an unintelligible mumble.

Spreading her hands above the warmth of the paraffin heater, Hilary said, 'You know *not* moving on every few days is going to seem rather dull. This trip has brought out the gypsy in me. Good morning, Richard.'

'Good morning.' He came to stand by the stove but kept his hands in his pockets.

'I was just saying to Nicola that I'm getting used to being in perpetual motion, but perhaps you've had enough and will be glad to stay put.'

'I shan't be staying put for long. I have to fly to New York early next week. My normal life is fairly mobile.'

'My everyday life is extremely settled and orderly,' said Hilary. 'Which is why I choose adventurous holidays. Will you be glad to get back, Nicola?'

'You're talking as if it were over,' said Nicola. 'There's still Pamukkale to see...and another night on the train...and Topkapi and the Grand Bazaar.'

'Who knows?' said Richard. 'Our second look at Istanbul could be the high spot of the trip.'

As he spoke, he looked at her mouth. It was almost as if he had leaned across the stove and kissed her.

The most direct route to Pamukkale had been blocked by heavy snowfalls, Serif reported. The alternative route would take longer.

For Nicola it was a morning of intense visual pleasure. There had not been many really white winters in her lifetime. When snow had fallen thickly, it had never stayed immaculate for long. In London it quickly turned to unpleasant grey slush. Even in the country town where she had grown up, roads were salted and swept, pavements and pathways shovelled, the illusion of a changed world lost.

But here, once they had left the main highway to follow the detour, they entered a Christmas-card world where it wouldn't have seemed surprising to see a Dickensian stage-coach coming in the opposite direction.

After driving from eight until eleven at a much slower speed than usual, they came to a small town where Nuray announced a coffee stop.

'Who would have expected to find a cake shop in these backwoods?' said Hilary, looking with surprise at the

range of confectionery in the glass display counter as
Serif shook hands with the proprietor.

'Here the best drink is *salep*,' he told her, putting one
arm round her shoulders and the other round Nicola's.
'Shall I order it for you?'

'What is *salep*?' asked Hilary.

'We drink it in winter to keep out the cold...and to
cure colds. It's made from the root of a wild orchid
mixed with hot milk and sprinkled with cinnamon...
delicious.'

Both women agreed to try it, but when, a few minutes
later, Nicola took a sip from her cup, she found it un-
bearably sweet.

The café had tables for four and she and Hilary were
sitting with Stuart and Lorna. Richard was at the table
alongside theirs and, although she had kept her reaction
to the drink to herself he leaned over and murmured,
'Not nice?'

'Too sweet for my taste.'

'Have my coffee.'

Without waiting for her assent, he exchanged her cup
for his.

'But you may not like it either,' she protested.

Leaning across for the second time, his hand on the
back of her chair, he said in her ear, 'Anything your lips
had touched would taste like nectar to me.'

It was obviously meant as a joke, but although she
smiled and said lightly, 'That sounds like one of Serif's
lines,' she was aware of another, deeper response.

If he could make her quiver when he was being fa-
cetious, how would she react to serious love-talk? But
perhaps there wouldn't be any. Perhaps he was one of
those men who, when making love, carefully avoided
saying anything which might be construed as
a commitment.

* * *

The journey continued across a great plain ringed by mountains. Most of the way they had the road to themselves. The few cars they saw had chains on their wheels.

Presently they came to a vast and desolate-looking lake. By now the back of the truck was thickly coated with snow thrown up by the rear wheels. Soon, in spite of the heater, the side-windows began to ice over. Deprived of a view, the more restive members of the party began to grumble.

For Nicola, music was an effective antidote to boredom. She and Richard had swopped cassettes and she spent the rest of the morning listening to his tape of Beethoven's Fifth and trying to make up her mind what to do about him when they reached Istanbul.

It was late afternoon when they came to Pamukkale, an immense petrified waterfall thousands of years old.

As the truck chugged up the hill alongside the great white cascade which had already been visible from several miles away, Nuray explained what it was.

'At the top of the hill are the ruins of ancient Hierapolis. Among them is a spring. The water is full of calcium bicarbonate. As it flows over the edge of the plateau, carbon dioxide is given off and the calcium carbonate turns to hard chalk...travertine. In summer this is one of Turkey's biggest tourist attractions. To save it being damaged, shoes are forbidden on the terraces. If you want to explore them, you must do it with bare feet.'

'Is the travertine slippery?' Janet asked.

Nuray shook her head. 'It may look like ice but you won't slip, and the water is warm.'

After paddling in the shallow pools on the cascade, they swam in the warm water of what had once been a sacred pool and was now a public swimming-bath surrounded by attractive semi-tropical gardens. Scattered on the floor of the pool were columns and blocks of stone, the remains of a large portico.

'Nicola...what have you done to yourself?' Hilary exclaimed, as they came out of the water together.

Nicola looked at blood trickling down her right leg. 'Oh, dear...how did that happen?'

'You must have grazed yourself on one of the submerged pillars.'

'It's nothing much. I didn't even feel it.'

In the changing-room she mopped up the blood with a tissue and stuck a plaster over the small laceration. Then she dried and dressed, but left off her jeans in case blood oozed through the plaster and stained them.

Leaving the baths with her towel wrapped like a sarong round her hips and thighs, she encountered Richard.

'What did you think of it?' he asked. 'I found it rather unpleasant...like swimming in soup. But I've never much cared for jacuzzis. Although maybe, if the Pera Palas has private spa tubs, I'd enjoy relaxing in one with you. How do you feel about that?'

# CHAPTER TEN

THERE was an electric pause. Nicola felt mentally pole-axed by the unexpected proposition.

Richard was looking down at her, and for once she *could* read his mind. He was visualising her lying in a bubbling spa tub in the luxurious bathroom of his hotel in Istanbul.

She hadn't expected to have to commit herself yet. The two sides of her nature—the rational and the reckless—were still locked in subconscious conflict. She was no nearer a decision than she had been several days ago.

'Hilary says you've hurt yourself, Nicola,' said Miles, from behind her.

She turned. 'It's nothing serious. Perhaps water at ninety-five degrees desensitises one's nerve-ends. I didn't feel a thing.'

'All the same, it would be a good idea to put some antiseptic on it,' said Richard.

When they got back to the truck, he insisted on removing the plaster to have a look at the place. Then he covered it with a better plaster from his own first-aid pack.

For a few minutes they had the truck to themselves, the others still being in the baths or on their way to the café.

'You haven't answered my question,' he reminded her. 'This trip has been fairly spartan. Shall we reward ourselves with a spot of *grande luxe* at the Pera?'

He made it sound like a decision to splurge on a bottle of champagne rather than ordering tea. Surely he must know that, for her, it was far more momentous? Perhaps not. Perhaps he was used to girls who didn't make a big deal out of this kind of proposition.

To her astonishment, she heard herself saying, 'Why not?' and then, 'But isn't the Pera Palas likely to be fully booked?'

'Not in February. Anyway, I already have a booking. I'll call them tonight from the station and tell them there'll be two of us.'

Serif put his head inside the truck. 'We must leave the station soon. Have you seen Nuray? I'd better find her.'

'After wearing trousers for nearly a fortnight,' said Nicola, 'I'm beginning to forget what it feels like to wear tights and a skirt.'

She stepped into her jeans and pulled them up under the towel before discarding it. 'Will jeans be all right at the Pera Palas? I didn't bring any smart clothes.'

'Nor did I. If we don't pass muster for the dining-room, we'll get room service to feed us.'

The train was already standing at the platform in the station at Denizli.

'This time we have three compartments reserved for us. With only four people in each, you'll be more comfortable,' said Nuray. 'I've put Hilary, Janet, Nicola and Sylvie together. In the men's compartment are Miles, Richard, Philip and Stuart. I am sorry to separate you, Stuart and Lorna, but it's only for one night. Lorna and I will be sharing with Bob and Joan. You won't mind being the only man with three women, will you, Bob?'

'Nothing I'd like better, love.' He cleared his throat. 'And now the moment has come to say thank you, on behalf of us all, to our driver. We've had a few hairy moments but here we are, safe and sound at the end of a very enjoyable trip, and we'd like to show our appreciation of the way you've looked after us, lad. Don't spend it all on lion's milk.'

Clapping Serif on the shoulder, he handed him an envelope containing the group's contributions to Serif's tip.

'It's very kind of you. Thank you. I've enjoyed the trip too,' said Serif, putting the envelope inside his leather jacket.

Later, after several people had taken group photographs, and everyone had supplied themselves with snacks and bottles of water from a kiosk on the platform, he shook hands with the men and kissed the women on both cheeks.

Soon after the train had pulled out of the station, it stopped at a smaller station where a boy was grilling chunks of meat over a charcoal brazier. As Nicola and Janet watched, a passenger from the train appeared with a large *pide* loaf which the boy filled with ten or twelve meat-laden skewers.

'I wonder what's on the menu in the dining-car?' said Janet.

'You were going to travel first class on the way back,' Nicola reminded her.

'Miles dissuaded me.' A few minutes later, when both Hilary and Sylvie had left the compartment, Janet said, 'Do you remember what else I said to you?'

'Remind me.'

'I said if one wanted to meet interesting men it was no use going on a cruise or to one of the luxury resorts because men men like doing uncomfortable things like rafting and trekking. I was right, wasn't I? Philip's a dead loss, but Miles and Richard are both worth a bit of suffering, wouldn't you say?'

'They're interesting men,' Nicola agreed.

'Come off it,' said Janet. 'Richard's a real prize. I would have bagged him for myself, but I'm not his type. At first I thought Nuray was, but now it's obviously you he fancies. I don't suppose you need warning that he probably isn't serious. But it'll be great while it lasts.

Even if Richard had been a possibility, I'd still have gone for Miles. There's a lot to be said for an older man, especially if he's in good shape, which Miles is.'

'But what about Hilary?' said Nicola.

'What about her?'

'She likes him too.'

'I'm sure she does. He's an attractive man...too attractive to settle for her. I'm not saying she isn't a nice woman, but sexually she's long past her sell-by date.'

Nicola's affection for Hilary made her resent this casual dismissal of her friend's claims to Miles's interest. But Hilary's return put an end to the conversation. It left Nicola disturbed and worried.

In her opinion, Hilary was a far more suitable partner for Miles than Janet. Miles would have to be out of his mind not to realise that.

As perhaps I am out of mine, she thought anxiously.

Later, stretched in her bunk, listening to the rattle of the wheels carrying them back to Istanbul, she flicked on her torch to check the time by her watch.

This time tomorrow she would be in bed with Richard. He would probably be asleep after making love to her.

Would she also be asleep? Or lying awake regretting her decision to join the list of his girlfriends?

She woke to find herself alone in the compartment with the other three couchettes returned to their daytime position.

She looked at her watch. Nine o'clock. The others must be having breakfast. Why hadn't they woken her? And why was the train still trundling through open country? Surely they should be back in Istanbul by now?

As she sat up and stretched, the door opened and Hilary held back the curtain screening the compartment from the view of passers-by.

'I thought you might like a glass of tea,' she said. 'You were so deeply asleep we decided not to disturb you. The train has been delayed by the snow. We'll be arriving late . . . much to the annoyance of those who are panting to go to the Grand Bazaar.'

'How kind you are...thank you.' Nicola took the glass and saucer. 'I couldn't get to sleep last night, hence my total torpor this morning. Did you sleep well?'

'I don't think anyone did.' Hilary sat down on the opposite seat. 'At least the delay means our rooms should be ready for us. I'll have a hot shower before I go to the bazaar. What about you?'

It was on the tip of Nicola's tongue to tell her she wouldn't be going back to the hotel with the rest of them. But something made her keep silent. Perhaps the feeling that Hilary would disapprove and hence a desire to postpone the loss of her good opinion until the last possible moment.

No one could accuse the older woman of being narrow-minded. Her tolerance had been demonstrated many times during the trek. At the same time it had been clear that she didn't like some modern manners and morals and wasn't afraid to say so.

As she was under the impression that Richard and Nicola had met for the first time a fortnight ago to-morrow, Hilary was bound to think it impetuous, if not lax, for Nicola to be spending the weekend with him.

When Hilary had gone, she dressed and dealt with the couchette. Luckily the conductor was in the corridor and she made signs asking him to lock the compartment while she went to the washroom.

When she returned, he had disappeared. She was wondering whether to wait or go in search of him when Richard appeared at the end of the corridor.

In the moments it took him to reach her, she made a decision.

'Locked out?' Richard asked. 'I'll go and find the conductor for you.'

'No...wait. I want to speak to you...privately. There may not be another chance.'

He raised an eyebrow. 'Changed your mind?'

'Not completely.'

'What does that mean?'

'I...I've decided I'd rather the rest of the group didn't know about... our arrangement. So I'll spend tonight with them and join you tomorrow.'

He received this announcement in silence. After a pause, he said, 'As you wish. In that case, shall I invite Miles and Hilary to join us for dinner?'

'That's a good idea.'

Her first reaction was relief that he wasn't annoyed. But when he had gone to find the conductor, it struck her that for him to accept the change of plan so easily showed that becoming her lover was far less important to him than to her.

The conductor came back and unlocked the door. When Nicola was in the compartment, Richard stood in the doorway and said, 'I don't want you to do anything you're not happy with, Nicola. If you'd rather not come to the Pera, you have only to say so.'

Perversely, now that he was offering her an escape, she felt as if something wonderful were about to be snatched away.

'Are you having second thoughts?' she prevaricated.

Richard glanced along the corridor in the direction of the dining-car. Then he stepped into the compartment and took her in his arms.

'Does that answer your question?' he asked, a few moments later, releasing her.

Her lips tingling from the unexpected and passionate kiss, she could only nod.

'But you haven't answered mine,' he reminded her. 'That you don't want the others to know about us suggests you aren't entirely comfortable with our arrangement.'

'I just don't feel it's their business. I prefer being discreet about these things.'

'Do you do "these things" often?' he asked.

Before she could reply, Janet appeared in the corridor behind him.

'What a bore this delay is. I was planning to dump my kit at the hotel and take a taxi to Ataköy Galleria, the new shopping mall. It sounds more my style than a bazaar full of tourist tat. Would you like to come with me, Nicola?'

'I'm not sure. I'll see what Hilary is planning. Excuse me, I'm going for breakfast.'

Richard had already stood aside for Janet to enter the compartment. Nicola avoided his eyes as she passed him. She needed time to compose herself after that vigorous demonstration of his attitude to their time together. She hoped he wouldn't follow her to the dining-car.

To her relief he didn't, and the rest of the group were filling in the AA questionnaires and didn't notice her sitting down at an unoccupied table for two.

Her breakfast had been served and she was drinking another glass of tea and looking at the snowy landscape when Nuray brought her a questionnaire.

'May I join you for a few minutes?'

'Of course, Nuray. You must be looking forward to being back with your family and having a few days' rest, aren't you? When do you start your next trek?'

'I have a new group arriving on Monday, on the same aircraft that you and Richard will be going home on. But they'll be doing a different trek. I shan't be repeating this one until next month.'

After signalling to the waiter to bring her another glass of tea, she said, 'Normally on Sunday I take the people who have booked the weekend in Istanbul on a boat trip along the Bosporus to the Black Sea. But Richard says that, as there are only the two of you, he thinks you can manage without me. Are you happy with that arrangement?'

Nicola nodded. 'You ought to have one full day off between treks. The company work you hard, don't they?'

Nuray smiled. 'Most people think my job is all holiday.'

'There's a lot of responsibility involved. When are you likely to be visiting your sister again?'

'It depends how busy the company is. Sometimes there aren't enough bookings and a trek is cancelled. May I have your telephone number? I'd like to visit the bookshop where you work and say hello to you.'

'We could have lunch together.'

'What was it like in the women's part of the *hamam*?' asked Richard, when he and Miles met Hilary and Nicola for drinks in the lobby before going out for dinner that evening.

The two women looked at each other and laughed.

'Interesting!' said Hilary. 'The building was fascinating architecturally, but we were rather less keen on the ministrations of the masseuses—especially the rubdown with an abrasive glove. If I went again, I'd buy a new *kese* beforehand. The ones used on Nicola and me looked as if they had abraded a lot of bodies. How was it for you two?'

'We had the place to ourselves. Miles had the chief masseur and I had his assistant,' said Richard. 'Apparently it's not done for men to strip off completely. We were issued with a loin cloth called a *pestamal* and a pair of wooden clogs which weren't too easy to walk in.'

Nicola said, 'We were given a towel later on, but nothing like your *pestamal*. Turkish women kept their briefs on.'

'We could have done with our own shampoo,' added Hilary. 'The brand they use in the *hamam* stings when it gets in your eyes. I thought it was like being shampooed by a friendly gorilla, didn't you, Nicola?'

'It was certainly *nothing* like the aromatherapy treatments my godmother gave me the Christmas before last. But I wouldn't have missed it. What did you think of it, Miles?'

He had been looking in the direction of the lifts. Now, instead of answering her question, he suddenly rose to his feet. 'I've asked Janet to join us,' he said. 'Here she comes now.'

During the afternoon, Janet had had her hair done.

'How do you like my new outfit? I bet there was nothing like this in the Grand Bazaar,' she said, showing off a quilted gilet and matching skirt of velvet-soft caramel suede, worn with a paler silk shirt. She had also bought a bronze bag and shoes.

Although she looked very smart, Nicola found it hard to believe that quiet, kind and seemingly wise Miles could be more taken with her than with Hilary. Which just went to show that physical attraction could warp any-one's judgement, she thought uneasily.

'I'm looking forward to seeing the Topkapi Palace to-morrow morning,' said Hilary, while they were undressing.

There was nothing in her cheerful manner to betray that she might be hurt by the fact that all evening Miles had allowed Janet to monopolise him.

'How fast this fortnight has flown,' she went on. 'I can't believe that this time tomorrow I shall be back in my own bed.'

And I shall be in Richard's, thought Nicola, with mingled anticipation and apprehension.

The pear-shaped Kasikci diamond was said to have been found in the rubble of the Blachernae Palace by an im-poverished spoonmaker who sold it for a few *lira*.

Now flashing and glittering in the light of a concealed spotlight, it lay on a bed of black velvet which rocked gently back, forth and sideways to show off the bril-liance contained in the huge stone.

Displayed on its own in a large alcove, protected by a pane of thick glass and probably by a sophisticated alarm system, the eighty-six-carat diamond and the rest

of the treasure amassed by the Ottoman sultans made
the jewellery in Bond Street shop windows seem like mere
trinkets.

In other circumstances, Nicola could have spent all
day feasting her eyes on the inspired designs and superb
workmanship of what had to be the world's most magnificent collection of jewels.

But these were not the only things Nuray wanted them
to see before, at noon, the rest of the group left for the
airport. And although Nicola had been looking forward
to this visit to Topkapi Palace, now she was here she
found it hard to concentrate on the wonders of the
sultans' domain when, in a few hours' time, she and
Richard would be alone at the Pera Palas.

It was a very cold day. The museum attendants were
wearing dark blue overcoats and standing close to radiators, although these did little to raise the temperature
in the vast kitchens where meals for the five thousand
inhabitants of the palace had once been prepared and
which now housed wonderful displays of Chinese celadon
and Japanese porcelain.

On the way to the most famous part of Topkapi, Nuray
stopped to address them. 'The word harem means "forbidden". Today you'll be shown only a few of the four
hundred rooms. For centuries the harem here was a
mystery guarded by Sudanese eunuchs. It wasn't until
about thirty years ago that the compound was opened
to the public. At one time there were nearly seven
hundred female slaves in the harem, but many of them
used to die from diseases carried by vermin or from our
cold winters.'

They entered the harem by the Court of the Black
Eunuchs leading to the legendary Golden Road to the
*Selamlik*, the private quarters of the sultans.

As they moved through the empty rooms, once
crowded with hundreds of women, Nicola wondered
what it had been like to be brought here against one's

will and, perhaps, selected for the bed of a man one had never seen and might find repulsive.

At least it was by her own choice that tonight she would share Richard's bed. Even so, she couldn't pretend to feel totally sanguine about it.

When the coach taking the rest of the group to the airport had disappeared round the corner, Richard said, 'I'll organise a taxi.'

On the way to his hotel, she tried to look calmer and more relaxed than she felt. Why *was* she flustered? This was something other people did all the time without making a big deal of it. So why did it feel a major commitment to her?

She hadn't been nervous the first time she went away with Ian. Perhaps because she had thought he was her future husband. She didn't think that about Richard.

In fact she had no idea what his long-term intentions were, if indeed he had any. For all she knew this could be a two-night stand, after which he would say goodbye and erase her from his memory as effectively as he had before.

It was then, as the taxi sped over Galata Bridge to the modern side of the city where the luxury hotels and the embassies were located, that in a sudden flash of understanding she knew she was here because—no matter what he felt—she was in love with Richard.

And before she had come to terms with this realisation she was hit by a second stroke of enlightenment. She had been in love with him from the moment of setting eyes on him three years ago.

People said it couldn't happen; that you couldn't fall in love with a stranger. But it had happened to her. She could see it clearly now. She had walked into his office and recognised instantly that he was the man she had been waiting for, the man she could love for the rest of her life.

And her instinct had been right. The past two weeks had confirmed that he did have the qualities she admired, that he *could* be the love of her life. Apart from one small crucial detail. That he might never feel the same way about her.

'You're very quiet, Nicola.' He reached out and took one of her hands, giving it a slight squeeze.

'I—I was thinking about the others...wondering if their flight would take off on time.'

'I liked Miles and Hilary. The rest...' He shrugged.

The taxi drew up outside the imposing green façade of the Pera Palas, and the other members of the group were driven from Nicola's mind by the likelihood that the next thing on Richard's agenda might be to make love to her.

The lift must have been installed when the hotel was built in 1892. Flanked by potted palms in brass urns on ornate torchères in the form of elephants' heads, it had an elaborate wrought-iron gate. Inside it was panelled with dark wood and equipped with a small sofa.

'Later I'll show you the room Kemal Atutürk used when he stayed here. They've made it into a museum,' said Richard, as they were borne upwards. 'This place has an interesting guest list. As well as kings, queens, maharajahs and several prime ministers, they've looked after Mata Hari and Sarah Bernhardt, Josephine Baker and Garbo, and of course Agatha Christie.'

The porter carrying Nicola's kitbag had Richard's key. He unlocked a door on the second floor. But the room into which he led them wasn't a bedroom but a spacious and comfortable, if rather old-fashioned, sitting-room. As the porter disappeared into an adjoining room, Nicola went to one of the windows. It had a fascinating view of the Golden Horn.

When she turned round Richard was tipping the porter. As the door closed behind him, Richard took off his windcheater and tossed it on to a chair. He beckoned her to him. 'Do you realise it's more than twenty-four hours since I kissed you?'

She went to him, trembling inside. Was this it? Was this the beginning of having all her dreams realised ... or shattered?

He took her face in his hands. 'Have you wanted this as much as I have ... to be alone together?'

'Yes.' Her heart was pounding so hard that she felt sure he must hear it.

As he bent his head she closed her eyes.

She was in his arms on the sofa when there was a tap at the door.

'I ordered some coffee.'

Gently, Richard disengaged himself and went to admit a waiter carrying a tray.

To Nicola's relief, the man didn't look at her as he placed it on a low table. Not that she was dishevelled, but she felt it must be obvious that his knock had interrupted a passionate embrace.

When the waiter would have poured out the coffee for them, Richard said something which stopped him. With an obsequious bow and a magician's dexterity in palming the tip, he whisked himself out of the room as swiftly and silently as his colleague.

'You've learnt far more Turkish than I have,' she said, watching Richard fill the cups.

'You forget ... I don't need much sleep. It was a distraction at night when I was trying not to think about you. But I shan't be improving my Turkish vocabulary tonight,' he added, handing a cup and saucer to her.

'Thank you.'

He picked up the other cup. Instead of returning to the sofa, he removed himself to an armchair a few yards away.

'If we're going back to the bazaar, I had better keep my distance. There's a Turkish proverb which says that

the longer a pleasure is postponed, the more intense it
becomes. It may be true.'

She was tempted to say, Let's forget the bazaar. Let's
go to bed. It was what part of her wanted; the secret
side of her nature which had always been controlled and
repressed by her more decorous side.

But her decorous side was still dominant, making her
answer lightly, 'I'd better get my things unpacked. I'll
take my coffee through to the bedroom.'

He rose to open the door for her, but he didn't follow
her in.

The bedroom was as spacious as the sitting-room,
dominated by a large double bed, the floor spread with
fine Turkish carpets. Her kitbag had been placed on a
luggage rack. She unlocked the padlock.

As she began distributing her belongings, she wondered what her father and mother would think if they
could see her now; what Gina would think.

There wasn't much doubt about her parents' reactions. They might not be shocked, but they would be
concerned. They wouldn't want her to be hurt.

Gina would be aghast. She knew from the photographs of Richard in the book trade Press that he was
attractive. But she would find it incredible that, having
professed to loathe him for the past three years, Nicola
could undergo a dramatic volte-face and, after only two
weeks, end up in bed with him.

I ought to tell him who I am, she thought, as she took
her washbag to the bathroom. I should have told him
before.

Compared with yesterday's group visit to the Grand
Bazaar, exploring the labyrinth of covered streets and
narrow alleys with Richard was a much richer experience.

He had a good-humoured way of dealing with the
salesmen who, whenever anyone paused to look at
their wares, immediately started a spiel in the appro-
priate language.

Even today, when the most luxurious shops were located elsewhere, it was easy to visualise the time when heavily veiled women had come here to choose silks and pearls from the Orient and be shown the latest innovations from the West.

At the heart of the maze was Ic Bedestan, the old bazaar, a survival from the fifteenth century with small cave-like shops filled with rugs, camel bells, brass platters, antique tiles and old silver.

In the street of the quilt-makers, Richard chose two beautiful hand-stitched quilts to be shipped to his sister in Boston.

Afterwards they found their way to the smaller Spice Bazaar where the familiar scents of vanilla and cloves mingled with more exotic seasonings. Nicola noticed a jar labelled 'Aphrodisiac des Sultanes' and wondered what was in it, and if Richard had noticed it. She was grateful to him for not rushing her to bed at the first opportunity, as Ian had. She had enough misgivings about this weekend already without being made to feel like a latter-day odalisque.

They had a late lunch at a restaurant up some stairs near the entrance to the spice market. It had been recommended to Richard by a friend who lived in New York and there were several Americans eating there.

'If we'd had more time,' he said, as they finished their meal, 'We could have taken a ferry to the Princes' Islands. They're only an hour or two offshore. One of my mother's forebears spent a couple of years in Turkey with Sir Henry Bulwer, who was British Ambassador here in the 1850s. He bought the island called Yassiada and built a castle there. Travelling and living abroad must have been a lot more interesting then than now.'

'Apart from my great-grandfather who served in France in World War One, I don't think any of my forebears ever set foot out of England,' said Nicola. 'Even my parents aren't keen on going abroad. They've never been further afield than the Highlands of Scotland and the west coast of Ireland.'

'Sensible people...they know what they like and stick to it. Half the people who travel today don't really want to see the world. They're just keeping up with their neighbours, or going one better,' he said. 'You can bet your life Bob and Joan will be glad to get home this afternoon. So will Lorna and Sylvie. They'll all be delighted to get back to the telly, and sliced bread, and cornflakes for breakfast.'

'At least Sylvie now knows that olives can be black as well as green,' said Nicola.

They both smiled at the memory of Sylvie helping herself to olives at breakfast one morning, under the impression that they were cherries, and reacting with her usual disgust to the unexpected taste.

Signalling to the waiter, Richard said, 'Shall we go back to the hotel now?'

# CHAPTER ELEVEN

LESS than half an hour later they were back in his suite.

'Siesta time,' he said, closing the outer door. While collecting the key from the porter's desk, he had asked for a bottle of Veuve Clicquot to be sent up.

'I'd like a shower,' said Nicola.

'Why not have a tub...more relaxing? I'll bring you a glass of champagne. Drinking chilled wine in a hot bath is my sister's favourite way of unwinding.'

'It sounds good.'

In the bedroom she unlaced her walking boots. Her fingers were trembling slightly and her heart was beginning to beat in slow, heavy thumps.

In the bathroom she turned on the taps and started to undress. Unlike some of the hotels they had stayed at during the trek, the Pera Palas didn't expect its guests to restrict their ablutions to certain hours. Steaming water gushed from the hot tap.

Noticing the various freebies included a small bottle of bubble bath, Nicola unscrewed the top and tipped the contents into the cascade. Normally she didn't like foam baths, preferring fragrant oils which left her skin feeling silky. But at this stage of the relationship she needed the screen of bubbles to help her through the initial awkwardness of being naked.

Perhaps Richard would think her absurdly shy, even prudish. Prudish she wasn't, but shy—yes. Given her limited experience, how could she not be?

Instead of using the shower cap provided—did anyone look good in a shower cap?—she clipped her hair high on the crown of her head, and stepped into the still filling bath.

She had turned off the taps and the bubbles were frothing round her shoulders, concealing the rest of her body, when there was a tap at the door.

'Come in.'

Richard came in, a glass of champagne in each hand, and shouldered the door shut behind him. 'I've hung the Do Not Disturb notice on our door and told the switchboard we aren't taking calls,' he said, as he handed one of the glasses to her.

'Nobody knows I'm here. Are you expecting any calls?'

'No, and it's not likely anyone will call, but some people do know I'm here. Before I came away, I didn't foresee that on——' he checked the date by his watch '—February the eighth I'd want to be incommunicado.' He sat down on the edge of the bath, by her feet. Lifting his glass, he said, 'To Amazing Adventures, and to my friend Sam, without whom I wouldn't have met you.'

It was her cue to say, 'Well, actually we've met before, but you don't remember it.' But this wasn't the moment. She would tell him later... afterwards.

'To Amazing Adventures.' She took a swig of champagne, hoping it would slow her pulse-rate.

Richard ran a hand over his jaw. 'Would you mind if I shave while you're in there?'

'Go ahead.'

He took his glass to the basin at the far end of the bathroom. As he took off his shirt, his tanned back rippled with muscle. She felt her insides contract. What was she worrying about? Whatever the outcome of this weekend, she was here with this gorgeous man. Very soon she would be in his arms again. Forget the past. Don't think about the future. Enjoy the here and now.

'Like some music?' Richard asked.

She hadn't noticed before that the bathroom had a radio.

'Yes, please.'

When he switched it on, two Turkish male voices were having what sounded like an argument. He found a station playing western orchestral music.

'How's that?'

'Fine . . . lovely.' After a pause she added, 'Your sister's prescription works.'

It wasn't, strictly speaking, true, but she could see that it would work . . . for ordinary tensions. Surprised to see him lathering his chin the way her father did, she said, 'I thought you'd use an electric razor.'

'I was expecting to stay at *pansiyons* which might not run to shaver plugs.' He looked at her through the mirror. 'I have a fairly stiff beard. I don't want to rough up your skin.'

She sipped her champagne and watched the swift, practised movements and steady hands with which he removed the creamy soap from the taut brown planes of his cheeks and chin.

'You'd be a good subject for a sculptor. You have the kind of head which translates well into bronze.'

He laughed, showing a flash of white teeth. Then his expression changed. In the act of rinsing his razor, he paused to give her a long look.

'And you should have sat for Renoir. You aren't as plump as most of his lovely ladies, but you look every inch as luscious.'

If his eyes had been teasing, she would have echoed his laugh. But they weren't. He sounded sincere. Luscious—me? she thought, startled. It wasn't a word she would ever have applied to herself.

Richard bent over the basin to sluice his face, neck and ears with handfuls of running water. When he straightened, his eyelashes were sticking together in spiky clusters, as if he had been swimming. She had a fleeting impression of the way he must have looked at eighteen.

Then he reached a long arm for one of the old-fashioned huckaback hand towels, with 'Pera Palas' woven into their borders. When his face was dry it became the one she was used to; that of a confident, worldly man who knew far more about women than she knew about men.

Whistling softly to the music, Richard spread tooth-paste on his brush. He sounded happy.

Damn right he's happy! What other mood d'you expect when you've fallen into his lap like a ripe plum...?

The voice in her head was her brother's.

Richard brushed his teeth, the movements of his hand and arm reactivating the exciting play of muscles on his back. He left the basin neat, folded the towel and drained his glass of champagne.

'More champagne for you?'

'Please.'

He left the room for a moment to fetch the bottle and ice-bucket. After refilling both their glasses, he put his on the floor next to the bath and then dabbled his hand in the bath water.

'More hot water?'

She nodded, sensing that he was playing with her, de-liberately postponing the moment all this was leading up to.

'Mind your feet,' he said, before turning on the tap.

She drew up her legs, her knees appearing like islands in the sea of foam. But his warning hadn't been necessary. The bath was a large one. She could have lain flat on the bottom with room to spare.

When he judged the temperature was right, he turned off the tap. Straightening, he unbuckled his belt.

'I'll come in with you ... if you don't mind?'

Although he amended the statement into a question, it was obvious he didn't expect a negative answer. Disconcerted—this wasn't what she had expected—she said nothing. She had dim memories of playing in the bath with Peter when they were both small, but had never shared a bath with an adult man.

Richard unzipped his jeans. 'Move forward, will you?'

As she sat up and edged forward, she was aware of a pair of long suntanned legs, of spilling some of her champagne, of the displacement of water as he slid down behind her, making the layer of foam quake and seem for a moment in danger of overflowing.

'Right...now you can lie back again,' he said, as the upsurge stabilised.

With one hand he retrieved his glass, with the other, spread over her midriff, he pressed her backwards until she was lying against his chest.

'How's that? Comfortable?'

'You're laughing at me.'

'No, no...I wouldn't do that.' She felt the vibration of his chuckle against her shoulder-blades. 'Well, yes...maybe a little. Why are you being so serious? We're here to enjoy...be happy together.'

He pressed a soft kiss on her temple, then gently nibbled the lobe of her ear. 'For me, this is the best part of the trip. Would you agree?'

She nodded, catching her breath as, under the water, his hand slid away from her waist and began to explore the rest of her body, starting with her breasts.

For a big man, he had an incredibly gentle touch. Nicola closed her eyes and let her head tilt back on to his muscular shoulder, her inhibitions evaporating as the slow movements of his fingers sent flashes of exquisite pleasure streaking along her nerves.

'I want to look at you,' he murmured presently, close to her ear.

Moments later she realised he must have opened the outlet with his foot. Beneath the foam, the water was draining away, leaving her covered with bubbles. As the bathwater ebbed, the foam began to evaporate. He accelerated the process by trickling some of his champagne over her breasts.

'Richard! It's cold!' she protested, not really minding.

He put the glass back on the floor, and hers with it. 'Turn around. I want to kiss you properly.'

She wriggled round to face him. They kissed. Suddenly it seemed the most natural thing in the world to be in his arms, in a bath, in a famous foreign hotel where princes and presidents had stayed. The only unnatural factor was not to be able to say, between kisses, I love you.

When Nicola opened her eyes on Sunday morning, she knew it was much later than her usual getting-up time.

Hardly surprising, she thought, smiling to herself.

Judging by the feel of Richard's body, curled round behind her, he was still deeply asleep.

That too had been predictable. After last night he might not wake up until noon!

She lay still, savouring the unaccustomed cosiness of sharing a bed, and remembering that first amazing hour after he had lifted her out of the bath, enveloped her in a large bath-sheet, carried her to bed and made love to her in a way she would never forget.

If only he had been her first lover, she thought wistfully. If only she had waited for him.

If only he could become her final and forever lover.

Quickly she pushed this thought to the back of her mind. The best way to live today was as if it were her last. One glorious butterfly-short span, worth more than a lifetime of mundane beetle-days.

'Nicola?' Richard's voice, soft but not drowsy, broke into her thoughts.

Without moving, she said equally quietly, 'I'm not asleep. I thought you were.'

As she spoke, he rolled on to his back, leaving her free to straighten her legs and stretch.

Last night, on his instructions, a waiter had used his pass key to open the outer door and wheel in a damask-clothed trolley while they were still in the bedroom. They had eaten in the sitting-room, wrapped in dry bath-towels. After a delicious light supper, and another bottle of champagne, they had come back to bed and made love . . . and made love . . . and made love. Until finally, exhausted by bliss, she had gone to sleep in his arms.

'What time is it?' she asked.

He reached out to take his watch from the night table. 'Almost nine-thirty. Time to make a move if we're going on that river trip.' He rolled back towards her, raising himself on one elbow to look down into her eyes. 'How did you sleep, lovely one?'

'Need you ask?'

Although, last night, he had swept aside her inhibitions, this morning she still felt a little residual shyness. Indeed now she had more to be shy about than before.

Last night she had startled herself. She had always known that, deep down, there was a wanton streak in her. But she hadn't expected it to surface quite so rapidly, so wildly.

He smiled. 'You were delicious . . . figuratively . . . literally . . . every way there is.' He bent to drop a kiss between her eyebrows. 'Let's brush our teeth and try out the shower. But first I'll order breakfast. What would you like?'

While he was calling room service, she couldn't resist running her hands over his smooth brown skin. Her touch wasn't intended to arouse him but it had that effect.

As soon as he had put the receiver back on its rest he began to return her caresses, his touch deliberately sensuous.

Suddenly last night's passion was flaring into new life. But this morning, unlike the first time, he didn't need to be gentle. Her desire was as urgent as his. Their bodies fused in a single swift fluid movement. Their hearts beat as one. They moved to the same eager rhythm, driving each other to the same breathless frenzy . . . sharing the same ecstatic free-fall.

\* \* \*

By the time they were ready to go out, the river mist seen from their room while they were breakfasting had cleared. The sun was shining.

On the advice of the helpful receptionist, instead of taking the two-hour boat-trip to the upper end of the Bosporus, where eventually it merged with the Black Sea, they took a taxi for the outward journey.

Although Richard talked to the driver most of the way, he also held Nicola's hand. From time to time he gave her looks which were hard to meet without revealing the full extent of her feelings.

The thought of a second night with him made her heart lurch in her chest.

Then she remembered that this time tomorrow they would be airborne for London, and on Tuesday he was flying to the States. For all she knew, the delights he had shown her last night might, for him, be a commonplace experience. What had seemed to her exceptional and wonderful might, in his life, be the norm.

They had lunch at a seafood restaurant on the water-front at Rumeli Kavagi on the European side of the strait. A Genoese fortress was visible on the Asian side, a fiddler was playing background music and pleasure boats, ferries, several cargo ships and even a winter cruise liner added interest to the scene. The other customers were mainly cheerful family parties of Istanbullus.

At this time of year the last boat back to the city left soon after three o'clock, but luckily it wasn't crowded. They found somewhere to sit with a good view of both shores.

'Two weeks ago today, we were on that other ferry,' said Nicola. 'I thought then it was Nuray you fancied.'

'And I thought you couldn't stand me,' Richard said drily. 'Talk about hostile vibes...'

It was a perfect opportunity to explain the reason for her initial hostility. She was about to do so when a man selling sweetmeats came up to them and Richard bought a box of *lokum*, the proper name for Turkish Delight.

The youth who was selling it wanted to practise his English and it was quite a long time before he moved on. By then Nicola had changed her mind, deciding to postpone her confession, if it could be called that, until she had some indication that this was a lasting relationship which had to be put on a straightforward footing.

If it was not going to last, what was the point of raking over the ashes?

The journey back was delightful. She felt sorry the rest of the group had missed it.

In places the Bosporus was wide, a mile and a half from bank to bank, both sides having castles and forts strategically placed on the heights above small clustered fishing villages and the painted or weather-bleached waterside summer-houses called *yalis*.

She wished Richard would put his arm around her. She was beginning to realise that, although she had loving parents and many friends, for a long time she had been starving for the special affection between a man and a woman. She wanted to take his hand and hold it to her cheek, to rest her head on his shoulder, to feel his arm round her waist.

But Richard, although he talked to her, was intent on the passing scene. She felt sure that, had he been in love with her, he would have been looking at her as often as at the view.

As soon as they got back to the hotel, he was as attentive and romantic as she could have wished, sweeping her back to bed and making masterful love to her.

But when he had gone for a shower, leaving her lying in a daze of satisfied languor, her doubts began to creep back. Surely, by now, if this was more than an affair, he would have given some hint of deeper feelings?

Later they dined at a small intimate restaurant famed for its Turkish cuisine but without a rigid dress code.

'My guest would like *bülbül göbegi*,' said Richard, when the head waiter asked if they wished for a sweet.

'I don't even know what it is,' she said, a few moments later.

'It's a nightingale's nest,' he said, smiling. 'Not a real one . . . it's made from *kadayif*, which I know you like, with pistachio nuts for the eggs. Wasn't I right? If you'd seen "nightingale's nest" on the menu in English, isn't it what you'd have chosen?'

She had to admit that it was. While she ate the nightingale's nest, Richard drank strong but unsweetened Turkish coffee.

Somehow she couldn't help feeling that the choice he had made for her and what he had chosen for himself might reflect the difference in their characters, and have a bearing in the nature of their relationship.

On the flight to England, Nicola assumed they would share a taxi to central London, one of them dropping the other off. It didn't work out that way.

Where the Customs hall debouched into the airport's main concourse someone from Barking & Dollis—a man she had never seen before—was waiting for Richard.

Apparently a crisis had blown up during the morning. Mr Kenton's mission was to brief Richard about it. He had come in a chauffeur-driven car and, when they reached it, said to her, 'You won't mind sitting in front, will you, Miss—er——? This matter is rather confidential.'

'Not that confidential, Kenton,' Richard told him impatiently. 'Miss Temple is the soul of discretion.' He smiled at her. 'Aren't you?'

Nicola said, 'I don't mind sitting in front if Mr Kenton wants to talk to you privately.'

The chauffeur was holding the rear door. Before Richard could argue, she opened the front one and got in. If they weren't going to be by themselves, it didn't really make much difference where she sat.

On the fast road through open country between the airport and the edge of the city, she retouched her lipstick, using the mirror attached to the back of the passenger's sun-visor.

As she'd hoped, it gave her a glimpse of Richard. He had started the trek with a tan and now, after two weeks of outdoor life, his face was strikingly bronzed compared with the office pallor of the man who had come to meet him.

But she also saw a subtle change from the way Richard had looked on the opposite side of the breakfast-table this morning, and in the seat next to hers on the flight. His relaxed expression had gone, replaced by a sterner mien. Now he looked more like the man who had sacked her three years ago.

Perhaps, as he listened grave-faced to whatever Mr Kenton was telling him, he was mentally passing sentence on someone else.

They were almost back in the metropolis when the glass panel opened and Mr Kenton instructed the driver to take the young lady wherever she wanted to go before returning to the office.

When the car stopped outside the house where Nicola lived, the driver got out to unlock the boot where her kitbag was stowed. As she got out, so did Richard.

'I'm sorry about this, Nicola.'

'It doesn't matter. I hope the trouble is nothing too serious.'

He shook his head, saying in a low tone the man in the car wouldn't hear, 'An in-house storm in a teacup, probably. But I'll have to sort it out before going Stateside tomorrow. I'll call you as soon as I can. Got your house key?'

She nodded, hating to have to say goodbye to him, especially in front of other people.

The driver was placing her kitbag on the doorstep. 'There you go, miss.'

'Thank you... and goodbye.' She bent to speak through the open rear door. 'Goodbye, Mr Kenton.' Straightening, she held out her hand. 'Goodbye,

Richard.' Her voice was husky as she added, 'And thanks for a marvellous weekend.'

He took her hand in his larger one. She had the feeling he wanted to sweep her into his arms and kiss her the way he had kissed her before leaving their room at the Pera Palas that morning.

But instead he lifted her hand to his lips.

'Thank you for sharing it with me. Take care of yourself.'

He stepped back inside the car. The driver closed the door and returned to his own seat. Richard looked at her through the window, his expression inscrutable, until the vehicle glided off. Then after a final wave he turned away to resume his conversation with Kenton.

She had been in the flat for ten minutes when the telephone rang.

'Hello?'

'Oh, good…you're back.' The voice was Gina's. 'How was the trip?'

'Fine. How are things with you?'

'Terrific! It's nearly knocking-off time. Shall I come round and bring you up to date?'

'Yes, do.'

'I'll be there in half an hour.'

By the time the doorbell rang, Nicola had been to the nearest shop to buy bread, milk, fruit and a bunch of early daffodils for the vase on the coffee-table. She had also flicked round with a duster, run the cold tap to clear the water in the pipe before filling the kettle and unpacked a jar of apple tea granules.

'You look wonderful,' said Gina, after hugging her. 'So how did things go between you and the Beast of B & D? Were you able to avoid him?'

'I'll tell you all that later. First tell me what's been happening while I've been away.'

'The main thing is that The Project is now public knowledge…the first two trade ads have appeared.' Gina delved in her tote bag and produced a copy of *The*

*Bookshop* and the tabloid-size *Bookworld News*. 'Here they are.' She opened both periodicals and laid them side by side on the coffee-table. 'Don't they look good?'

Nicola had already seen and approved the layouts designed for them by an ex-boyfriend of Gina's who worked for an advertising agency. But this was how they had been seen by booksellers up and down the country.

Her eyes skimmed the familiar text of the advertisement, every word of it carefully thought out, all the stale clichés of publishing avoided.

'Margaret's over the moon with excitement,' said Gina. 'Especially about the editorial feature, which she knows is worth ten advertisements. Look…how does that grab you?'

'They've used the photo!' Nicola exclaimed.

Another of Gina's contacts, an up-and-coming photographer, had taken the picture of Gina and Nicola sitting on either side of Margaret, all three of them beaming at the camera as radiantly as if Margaret's novel were already at No. 1 on the best-seller lists.

The article below the photograph not only filled the page but continued overleaf.

'You can read it properly later,' said Gina. 'Most of it's a rehash of my Press release with some editorial comments worked in. They also rang Margaret for quotes and, predictably, she sang your praises and said she would never have finished such a long, ambitious book without your encouragement…especially after B & D had rejected the outline she submitted to them.'

'I must call her,' said Nicola. 'Just to let her know I'm back.'

She picked up the telephone, dialled the number and had a short conversation with her excited author who, fired by their confidence in her, was now at work on another long novel.

'How about some coffee?' said Gina, when Nicola replaced the receiver. 'Now I look at you closely, you look a bit bushed. Did you have to crawl out of bed at an ungodly hour this morning?'

'Not specially. I've had some late nights. Instead of coffee, try apple tea.' Nicola had left Gina's parcel on the worktop near the kettle. 'Here's a small present for you. Nothing lavish, I'm afraid.'

Gina, who liked to make the most of her handspan waist, was delighted with the silver-buckled belt. 'I hope you bought something for yourself and didn't spend all your pennies on me.'

'I've got some Turkish beads, but they're still in my luggage.'

They took their mugs to the sitting area. Gina slipped off her loafers and made herself comfortable at one end of the sofa. 'So now tell about your trip...from the beginning. You said in your letter that Richard Russell hadn't recognised you. But that was only a few days into the trek. Did he cotton on later...or did you tell him who you were?'

'Neither...he still doesn't know.'

'Are you serious?' Gina exclaimed. 'How come?'

'There never was a good moment to bring it up and have it out.'

'He's going to know before long...as soon as he sees the trade papers. Did you have much to do with him? What sort of terms were you on by the end of the trip?'

Nicola had already debated whether to tell her friend how her time in Turkey had ended. But although she and Gina were close they had had too much else to talk about to spend much time discussing their love-lives in detail.

She said, 'Quite friendly terms actually. I...I changed my mind about him. That may sound strange after all the bad things I've said about him in the past, but when you're with someone every day from breakfast to bedtime you get to know them pretty well. He's a much nicer person than I imagined.'

'He's still the guy who sacked you,' said Gina. 'I don't understand how you could spend two weeks with him and not bring that up... not ask him to justify himself. You say by the end you were on "quite friendly terms". How friendly? Are you going to see him again? Did you exchange telephone numbers?'

'Everyone did. Whether Richard will call I don't know. He's off to America tomorrow. He'll be away for ten days. His brothers and sisters are there, apart from B & D's parent company.'

'Well, even if his *amour propre* is only half as sensitive as the average male ego, he's not going to like being made to look foolish,' said Gina, with a gesture at the trade periodicals.

'What do you mean? How does Richard come into it?'

'The fact that he sacked you is mentioned. It does add spice to the story from a journalistic point of view.'

'I'd better read what they've written.'

Nicola reached for *The Bookshop* and started reading the rest of the article which had appeared the previous Friday.

Margaret Wanstead's second novel *The Gothick Window*, to be published by Trio in simultaneous hardback and paperback in May, is a bold experiment by three women who, not long ago, were victims of the 'rationalisation' which left many publishing people redundant and some 'mid-list' authors without a publisher.

Margaret Wanstead and her editor, Nicola Temple, were both with Barking & Dollis until the advent of B & D's new CE, Richard Russell.

But although B & D weren't impressed by the outline of Wanstead's second book and waived their option on it, Temple was convinced the novel was a winner.

She and former PR-girl Gina Latimer, another victim of the recession, decided to pool their resources and publish the book themselves, calling their imprint Trio.

The story went on to describe the smallness of their initial investment, the big input of time and energy on top of their regular jobs, their problems with distribution and their innovative ideas about marketing.

It was first-class free publicity; but, as Gina had indicated, it wasn't going to please Richard.

Although it didn't go as far as to credit Nicola with statements she had never uttered, it was certain to leave everyone who read it with the feeling that he had blundered, and that a major part of her motivation was a determination to prove him wrong.

# CHAPTER TWELVE

NICOLA spent the following weekend with her parents. Soon after her arrival her mother said, 'You know that unpleasant man who sacked you from Barking & Dollis...?'

Nicola tensed. 'What about him?'

'There was an article on him in a bundle of magazines I was given for the white elephant stall at next month's coffee morning.'

Nicola tried to sound casual. 'Have you still got them?'

'No, I've passed them on to Mrs Finsbury who's running the stall.'

'Oh.' Nicola hoped her disappointment wasn't visible.

'But I cut the article out for you. It's in my desk. I'll fetch it.'

In her methodical way Mrs Temple had made a note of which magazine it came from and the date of the issue. The feature, part of a series on London's eligible bachelors, had appeared eighteen months ago.

'I know one can't believe all one reads, but it makes him sound a dreadful womaniser,' said Mrs Temple. 'I don't like that type of man. There's no such thing as a reformed rake, in my opinion. They can never resist another conquest, which makes life hell for their poor wives.'

It wasn't until after lunch, when she and her father had dealt with the washing-up, that Nicola was able to retreat to her room and study the article in detail.

With several small pictures of him escorting different but equally gorgeous girls, there was a large picture of him looking heartbreakingly attractive in a dinner-jacket.

Reading the text made it clear why the feature had increased her mother's dislike for him. But Nicola couldn't relate this image of Richard to the way he had been in Turkey.

She felt sure that Gina, who kept a close eye on all the glossies, would have known about the feature but decided to keep it to herself.

One result of the piece in *The Bookshop* was that a number of would-be writers having difficulty finding a publisher made contact with Nicola by writing care of the trade paper.

She also heard from several published authors who weren't happy where they were and thought she sounded more *simpatica* than their present editors.

But the one person she wanted to hear from remained silent. Although she knew he might be extremely busy, she had hoped he would find time to telephone her from America. But ten days passed and no call came.

She had been back at work for two weeks and was wondering if she ought to make contact with him when, on Friday evening, someone rang the downstairs doorbell.

As she wasn't expecting anyone, she felt sure it had to be him and hurried to use the entryphone.

'Who is it?'

'Richard Russell.'

Nicola's heart contracted. 'Come up. It's the top floor.' She pressed the button to unlock the street door.

Knowing it wouldn't take him long to reach her front door, she dashed to the bedroom to run a comb through her hair.

Richard's loud double rap on the door had something peremptory about it. When she opened the door and saw him standing on the landing, his forbidding expression confirmed her fear that he had been furious to find himself mentioned in the article in *The Bookshop*.

'Good evening.' His tone was formal. 'I hope it's a convenient moment to talk to you.'

'Of course...come in.' She stood aside so that he could enter. 'How was your trip to the States?'

Ignoring the question, he walked to the centre of the room, casting a cursory glance around her living quarters. Then, turning to face her, he said curtly, 'Why didn't you tell me who you were?'

It was a moment she had foreseen and mentally re-hearsed many times.

She said quietly, 'At first I thought you must know who I was. When I realised you didn't, it seemed more tactful to say nothing.'

'Tactful!' he exclaimed explosively. 'You lied to me...made a fool of me.'

She shook her head. 'That isn't true. I—I acted as I thought best...to spare us both embarrassment. What, really, was the point of dredging up our first meeting if you had no memory of it?'

'I suppose that depends on how highly one rates the truth. Clearly it isn't a matter of priority with you,' he said cuttingly.

His tone flicked her like a whiplash.

'I think my regard for the truth is as high as most people's. It was an awkward situation. Surely if anyone has a right to feel aggrieved it's me, not you.'

'How do you make that out?' he asked tersely.

'It is rather galling to discover that someone who's had a major impact on your life has absolutely no recol-lection of ever seeing you before.'

'So you took your revenge by making me look a fool in front of the entire industry.'

'That's neither fair nor true,' she protested. 'I was as surprised as you to find your name mentioned in the pieces about Trio in the trade Press. There was nothing about you in Gina's original Press release, apart from a reference to the fact that Margaret's first novel was pub-lished by Barking & Dollis who decided not to take up an option on her second book. It was the journalists who wrote those articles who dragged your name in.'

'Which doesn't exonerate you,' he told her coldly. 'Your deception might be forgivable if we'd remained no more than holiday acquaintances. But we didn't. Which makes your behaviour devious to say the least. I repeat ... you lied to me. That it was a lie by default doesn't make it any more acceptable.'

The bite in his tone made Nicola's temper start to simmer. 'I did *not* lie,' she retorted. 'I simply didn't remind you of circumstances most men of feeling would have remembered for themselves. To accuse me of lying is as wild an exaggeration as...as my saying you seduced me.'

'As to that, I'd be interested to know just why you agreed to spend the final two days at the Pera with me. In the light of what I've learned since, I don't think it was for the reason I thought at the time.'

'And what reason was that?' she asked.

He was silent for several seconds, his blue eyes slightly narrowed and locked with hers so that she found it impossible to look away.

'For love,' he said harshly. 'Love or lust are the usual reasons why people go to bed together. In Istanbul I assumed that, with you, it would have to be love.'

If, by the smallest hint, he had indicated any tender feelings towards her, she would have admitted instantly that his assumption had been correct.

But his judgemental frown was so like the man who had sacked her and so unlike her companion at the Pera Palas that she found herself saying in a flippant tone, 'You've missed out another reason ... curiosity.'

He looked momentarily baffled. 'Curiosity?'

'After reading a piece about you in one of the glossies, I couldn't resist finding out if you really were the great lover you were cracked up to be.'

Her riposte made a subtle change to the look on his lean face: the difference between hot anger and icy rage. She knew she had gone too far and had only herself to blame for whatever he did next.

'I see. And did I pass muster?' he asked, in a tone which made her quail inwardly.

When she didn't answer he crossed the space between them in a couple of strides and took her roughly by the shoulders. 'Come on...how did you rate me?'

'Richard...please...I wasn't serious.'

He misunderstood what she meant.

'Clearly! In which case it's just as well you were playing games with a well-known stud. A nicer guy could have been seriously hurt, thinking you might be serious about him.'

Bending his head, he kissed her hard on the mouth; a kiss of deliberate and brutal sensuality from which she instinctively recoiled as if it were a stranger trying to force a response from her.

At that moment he *was* a stranger, not the demanding but never ungentle lover he had been in Istanbul.

For a horrible moment she thought that, in this new guise, he might try to take her again and, in so doing, ruin every memory of that brief two-day idyll.

But, to her relief, he didn't. As suddenly as he had grabbed her, he let her go.

'It's all right. Don't panic,' he said sardonically. 'I've got the message. You only let your hair down on holiday...not on home ground.'

He stormed past her and was gone, banging the door behind him.

The following week she had a day off from the shop. She was reading a manuscript which had been forwarded to her when the doorbell rang. Could it possibly be Richard?

Full of hope, she dashed to the entryphone speaker. 'Hello...who is it?'

'Parcel post for Miss N. Temple,' said an unknown male voice.

Her spirits sinking back to the rock-bottom level which had been the norm since their row, she said, 'I'll be right down.

'Are you sure it's for me?' she asked, when the parcel turned out to be not another typescript but something large and heavy.

'If you're Miss N. Temple it is,' said the driver. 'Sign here, please.'

It wasn't until Nicola had dumped the parcel on the floor in her living-room that she saw that the stamps were Turkish. The only people she knew in Turkey were Serif and Nuray. Why should either of them send her a present?

Opening the parcel took several minutes. What it contained was a rug folded with its underside outwards. When she spread it out on the floor she recognised it as the expensive rug she would have bought had she been able to afford it.

In the centre of the rug was an envelope containing a note. 'For Nicola, from Richard—a memento of Kas.'

'Nicola! What's wrong?' Gina demanded, arriving for supper that evening and seeing at a glance that her friend had been crying.

Later, when Nicola had confided the whole story to her, Gina said, 'You know what you should do? Go to see him. The rug is a perfect excuse. In the circumstances you can't keep it. So return it to him...in person.'

'What good will that do?'

'He's had time to cool down...think things over. He may regret what he said, but not feel like making the first move. Men find it harder to say they're sorry than we do. Their upper lips are stiffer and so are their necks. If you appear on his doorstep looking fragile and wan, probably he won't just climb down...he'll jump down in one easy movement.'

'I doubt that,' said Nicola.

'It's worth a try, isn't it? As it's going to cost the equivalent of the taxi fare to his place to post the rug back to him, what have you got to lose?'

The following evening, with the rug rolled into a cylinder and fastened with plastic sticky tape, Nicola stood in the street waiting for a taxi.

It was a fine dry evening and under her coat she was wearing what, in Gina's opinion, was the most feminine outfit in her wardrobe: a honey-coloured dress with a nipped-in waist and full skirt.

'Go to town on your eyes, but go easy on the lipstick,' Gina had advised, the night before. 'You don't want to look as if your whole world has crashed, but you don't want to look cheerful either. And when he invites you in—only an arrant boor would grab the rug and slam the door—first off let *him* do the talking. I would guess he's been feeling a heel ever since he stamped out. Give him a chance to say so. Don't rush in and abase yourself first. What you did—or rather what you didn't do—wasn't so terrible.'

A taxi drew up alongside her and the driver jumped out and came round to the pavement. 'Let me give you a hand with that, love. Where do you want to go?'

Less than ten minutes later she was outside Richard's door, preparing to press the bell.

If he wasn't at home, Gina had advised repeating the visit until she did catch him in.

'If you're serious about the man, so what if it costs you money to get back together with him?' she had said.

However, it seemed that he was in because, as she waited for the door to open, she could hear music playing.

But it wasn't Richard who opened the door. It was a girl in the checked cotton trousers and starched white tunic of a chef.

Nicola knew instantly who she was. Her name was Jane Stonebridge. She was the daughter of a North

Country landowner and, after taking a cordon bleu course in Paris, she had started cooking for private parties.

She had been cited as Richard's latest *amour* in the article in the glossy.

'Hello,' she said, smiling. 'Richard's still in the shower. I'm Jane…the cook. Goodness, what an exciting-looking present——' her eyes on the rug. 'Come in. The party doesn't start until half-past eight, actually. But it doesn't matter that you're a little ahead of time. He's already opened the wine and he won't be more than ten minutes. He came home early tonight.'

It was not quite a quarter to eight. Nicola had checked the time in the taxi. But, although there might be a gap of half an hour between Richard's finishing dressing and the arrival of the first guests, this was not the time to confront him. Especially not in the presence of a former girlfriend, who might now be current again.

'Is it heavy? Shall I take one end?' the other girl asked.

'No, it isn't very heavy… and I'm only delivering it, not coming to the party.'

'Oh, I see.' Jane took charge of the parcel. 'Is there a card inside?'

'No, but he'll know who it's from. Actually it's not a present … just something I'm returning. Goodbye.'

Nicola turned and hurried away.

It wasn't until she got home that she wondered why she had been so stupid. By leaving the rug there, she had lost the only reason ever to see him again.

With her wits about her, she could have pretended to be looking for someone called Henry Jones and brought the rug away with her. If Richard had heard the doorbell and asked Jane who had called, she would have said, Someone with the wrong address.

At ten o'clock the telephone rang.

'Oh…you're home,' said Gina, when Nicola answered it. 'I hoped you'd still be out. What happened? How did it go?'

When Nicola told her, she said, 'That wasn't very bright, Nicola.'

'I know, but I was confused when the girl called Jane came to the door. They may be back together again. For all I know they may never have been apart.'

'The chances are she was there in her professional capacity. The magazine may have exaggerated his interest in her,' Gina said bracingly. 'Write a note to him now and post it first thing tomorrow. Say you were overwhelmed by his marvellous present, that you would have loved to keep it, but, knowing the way he feels about you, you felt that you couldn't. Explain about hoping to see him but not wanting to intrude on the party. Hey, I've got a better idea. Tomorrow, send him some flowers or a plant as a late birthday present. Then he'll have to make contact with you.'

'I can't do that,' said Nicola. 'It's too much like trying to ensnare him. If he wants me, he'll get in touch. He's not the shy, diffident type. Richard's a man who knows what he wants and goes for it. If he wanted me, he'd have been round here days ago.'

'I'm not so sure,' said Gina. 'Men are a very strange species. Some are tigers and some are pussycats, and sometimes falling in love turns a pussycat into a tiger and vice versa.'

'I'll think about it,' said Nicola.

'That's a large part of your trouble,' Gina told her. 'You think too much. If you could only bring yourself to do what comes naturally instead of endlessly analysing your feelings and speculating about his, you'd be a lot better off. Do you know what I'd do in your place?'

'What?'

'I'd ring him up—now!—and tell him how miserable I felt. Cry a little. Why not? What have you got to lose?

At worst he can only cut you off. At best he might rush round to comfort you.'

'Is it likely... in the middle of a party? I have a better idea. I'm going to do some work. It's work, not love, which really makes the world go round... and we aren't going to make our fortunes out of one book, however well it sells. So the sooner I get back to the slush pile the better.'

Her eyes went to the stack of unsolicited manuscripts waiting to be read.

'Goodnight, Gina. Thanks for your sympathetic ear. Don't worry; I'm not going to pine and die.'

# CHAPTER THIRTEEN

THE days that followed gave Nicola an uncomfortable insight into the reasons why people in deep depressions lost the energy even to get out of bed and get dressed.

There were several mornings when she felt like pulling the bedclothes over her head and staying where she was instead of facing another day at the shop. She still had her family and her friends, but the only person she really needed was Richard. Without him, the world was a wilderness and the future as terrifying to contemplate as being imprisoned for life.

Her unhappiness over Ian had been nothing like this. Even the trauma of being sacked had not been as bad, for then she had been sustained by anger and a sense of injustice.

What she was going through now was both deserved and self-inflicted. She had brought it on herself by her own lack of moral courage. No wonder Richard despised her.

The launch party for *The Gothick Window* was held at the Royal Over-Seas League.

The room booked for the party overlooked the garden at the back of the building and, beyond, the taller trees and open spaces of Green Park.

Nicola was the first to arrive. She hadn't seen Gina for a week although they had talked by telephone while Gina was shepherding Margaret round the provinces on a promotion tour.

It had had to be done on a shoestring because they didn't have the funds to do it in style like the major publishing houses. Instead of travelling first class on trains to the nearer cities and by air to the distant centres, they had done the trip by car.

It must have been quite exhausting, especially for Margaret, who wasn't used to rushing from place to place. But already it had produced some excellent newspaper and local radio interviews as well as valuable publicity on regional television chat shows.

The time on the invitation cards was six to eight-thirty p.m. After which Nicola and Gina would take Margaret and her husband out to supper.

Standing at one of the tall windows while, behind her, the League's staff put the finishing touches to the buffet table, Nicola looked out at the golden-green light of a perfect spring evening and wondered what Richard was doing.

Perhaps he was still at his desk, or striding homewards to change for a dinner party or a date. It might be that he wasn't in London at the moment. Wherever he was, he wouldn't be thinking of her.

Oh, God, how can I bear it . . . this terrible aching longing for him? she thought forlornly.

'Hi, there! How's it going?' said Gina, from behind her. 'Oh, don't you look nice . . . and so relaxed! I feel totally frazzled. Does it show?'

'Not a bit,' Nicola assured her. 'If you're frazzled, how about Margaret? Where is she?'

'In the Ladies' . . . changing. On our first day out she was nervous, but after that she enjoyed it. I was amazed at how well she handled the interviews. By the end of the week you'd have thought she'd been doing it for years.'

When she judged that all the guests who were important from a publicity point of view had arrived, Gina mounted a step-stool which made her visible to everyone in the crowded room and rang a small bell to claim their attention.

'Ladies and gentlemen, Margaret and Nicola and I would like to thank you for coming to what, for many of you, is just another publishing party, but for us is a very special occasion. Already we have grounds for believing that Margaret's book is going to be a big success.'

With justifiable pride, she announced the number of copies 'subscribed' by bookshops up and down the country.

She concluded her speech by saying, 'To borrow a phrase often used in authors' dedications, there is one person without whom none of this would have happened. His contribution to our new imprint, Trio, illustrates the truth of the proverb that it's an ill wind that blows no one any good.

'As most of you know, at the end of Eighties, the wind of change blew through the publishing world. For some of us it seemed an ill wind...a *very* ill wind. Actually, for Margaret, Nicola and me, that spell of adversity was good for us. It galvanised us into proving ourselves. It challenged us to tackle something we would never have attempted in the normal course of events. The first to feel the spur was Nicola and, for a while, the man who applied it wasn't her favourite person. But she feels differently now.'

Gina paused to look round her audience.

'Have you guessed who I'm talking about? Please join me in giving a warm welcome to one of the most dynamic influences in publishing and, in a way, the prime mover of Trio...Mr Richard Russell of Barking & Dollis.'

As Gina started to clap and other people followed suit, Nicola felt a wave of panic at the realisation that she was going to have to face Richard in front of all these people. Her second reaction was anger that Gina, and Margaret as well, had conspired to arrange his presence without consulting her. In those moments it seemed a unforgivable betrayal.

Then the people near her drew back to allow the unexpected guest to make his way to Gina's side. And the sight of him, taller and browner than any of the other men there, swept aside every thought but the joy of seeing him again.

She watched him shake hands with Gina before she stepped down from the stool. Richard did not take her place on it. He didn't need to. His height made him easily seen.

As the clapping died down, he said, 'Good evening, ladies and gentlemen. You're probably as surprised to see me here as I was to be invited. As Gina has indicated, to two of the principals of Trio I should be *persona non grata*. However, there are few publishers who haven't made similar errors of judgement. I'm very glad that in this instance my unwise decision to dispense with Nicola Temple's services has led to this happy occasion.'

He turned to smile at Margaret. 'Gina gave me an advance copy of Mrs Wanstead's novel, which I've read with great interest and enjoyment. It's a matter for regret that it isn't on Barking & Dollis's list. I haven't any doubt it will be extremely successful. Not only because it's being published with exceptional verve, but because anyone who reads it will want their friends to read it. As everyone in publishing knows, enthusiastic readers, especially if some of them are booksellers, can sell a book far faster than any amount of expensive hype.'

His blue eyes ranged over his audience. 'In my opinion too many second-rate books have been hyped as surefire best-sellers in recent years. But *The Gothick Window* is not, as we so often hear, written "in the tradition" of any established author. Margaret Wanstead has her own style and her own special view of the world.'

After a pause, he continued, 'One good book doesn't make a list, but a resounding success is a fine way to start. I'm sincere in wishing this new imprint well. It seems highly probable that—having already turned adversity to their advantage—Gina and Nicola are destined to do great things. There are not many people who, in similar circumstances, would have had the magnanimity to include me in these celebrations. My congratulations and best wishes to both of you and to your first publication.'

There was another burst of applause, curtailed when
Margaret mounted the stool and signalled that she had
something to say.

'Thank you for the nice things you've said about my
book, Mr Russell. I'd just like to add that if it weren't
for my editor, Nicola Temple, I might never have finished it. There were many, many times when I felt I had
bitten off more than I could chew. Nicola was an unfailing source of encouragement when I was tired, de-
pressed or having problems with my plot. I owe a
tremendous debt to these two remarkable girls. Thank
you both for everything.'

Blowing a kiss to Gina with one hand, and another
to Nicola with the other, she stepped down.

'Would you like to say something, Nicola?' Gina
asked, under cover of the clapping.

Nicola shook her head. 'You might have warned
me——' she began, in an undertone.

Gina didn't let her finish. She jumped back on the
stool. 'Right; that's the formal part over. Now I'm sure
most of you would like to meet our author, and, if
anyone here hasn't already received a complimentary
copy of *The Gothick Window*, please help yourself from
the stack on the table over there.'

As she began to introduce people to Margaret, Richard
turned to Nicola.

'That was a very nice compliment Mrs Wanstead paid
you.'

Even a close observer would have seen nothing in his
manner to hint at the rift between them.

'Yes, wasn't it,' she agreed. 'Let me get you a drink.'

But it was Richard who caught the eye of a waiter
circulating with a tray of wine and put a glass into her
hand before taking one for himself.

'To Trio!' he said, raising his glass.

'Thank you.' She lifted hers in acknowledgement.

How had Gina induced him to come? What was his
reason for coming? What was he really thinking behind

the urbane front he was putting on? Why couldn't she be equally civilised instead of standing here tongue-tied, unable to think of a single polite nothing to utter?

'Did you know I was coming?'

She searched for an evasive reply but failed to find one. 'Er...no...actually I didn't. But I'm very glad you're here.'

'Are you?' he said, his eyes sceptical. 'You look like someone who has read that, when unexpectedly confronted by a large and dangerous wild animal, the only thing to do is to stand one's ground.'

'Richard...how nice to see you again,' said Hilary, appearing beside them.

Discreetly made up, in a black dress with pearls round her neck and in her ears, and a beautiful antique paste brooch pinned to her shoulder, she looked more like an elegant Londoner than a green-fingered countrywoman.

'Hilary! Good to see *you*.' Richard bent to kiss her.

The three of them had been chatting for a few minutes when Miles came into view and, with him, Janet.


'Where's Richard?' asked Gina.

'I think he's gone.' Nicola surveyed the room. The party was thinning out now. 'I don't see him anywhere.'

'Gone? You mean you let him go?' her friend expostulated.

'We weren't together when he left.'

'You damn well should have been!' Gina said crossly. She lowered her voice. 'I didn't go to all that trouble to get him here for you to louse things up again.'

'What trouble? What are you talking about?'

'I delivered his invitation in person. I didn't make an appointment. I just showed up at B & D and sent in my card with "in partnership with Nicola Temple" scribbled on it. Although he had someone with him, I got the red carpet treatment. By the way, his secretary said how pleased she had been to read the piece about us in *The*

*Bookshop* because she remembered how shattered you'd looked the day he sacked you.'

At this point Gina broke off to say to some people on their way out, 'Thank you so much for coming.'

'When I was shown in to see him,' she continued, 'he couldn't have been nicer.'

'He usually is, I gather, with attractive women.'

'There are times, Nicola, when I could shake you,' Gina said, through clenched teeth. 'The man is in love with you. That's why he came tonight. Don't you realise what strength of character it took for him to come here and admit to a major error of judgement in front of all those people? It takes a real man to do that, and the reason he did it is because he's crazy about you.' .

'Did he tell you that?'

'Don't be a dope. Of course not. Men like Richard don't expose their deepest feelings to anyone but the woman they love—and you're not giving him any encouragement to tell you. Far from looking overjoyed to see him tonight, you looked as if a giant anaconda had just slithered in.'

As this tallied with Richard's description of her reaction, Nicola had to accept that she had looked markedly unwelcoming.

'It wouldn't surprise me if his reaction to this caper is to go home and get smashed out of his mind,' said Gina. 'Except that he isn't the type to drown his sorrows in Scotch. If you've any sense you'll go round there and tell him you thought it was wonderful of him to come tonight.'

'How can I do that? We're taking Margaret and Keith out to dinner.'

'I can cope with them on my own. Margaret will understand if I tell her you've got a headache. She's beginning to feel bushed herself. So am I. We shan't be making a night of it.'

Nicola hesitated. She still wasn't sure that Gina was right about Richard's motive for coming to the party. If she were, why had he left early?

Her friend read her mind. 'Look, I know you very well, and now I've met him and talked to him at some length. You're obviously made for each other. If you had the guts to launch Trio—it was *your* idea, remember?—what's stopping you saying that you love him? I mean, are women equal or aren't they? Do we still have to sit around twiddling our thumbs, waiting for men to stick their necks out? He's done that once— asking you to stay at the Pera Palas with him. This time why not stick *your* neck out?'

Nicola's mind was made up not by Gina's homily but by the realisation that if she didn't take a chance the future would remain a void of lonely nights and quietly desperate days. Her only joy would be work, and even that satisfaction would be diminished by the emptiness in her heart.

'I'll go. I'll try it,' she said, suddenly decisive.

Gina let her shoulders sag as if she had just accomplished an uphill task.

'And if he's not there,' she said, straightening, 'camp on his doorstep till he shows up.'

He was not at home when she arrived at his house. There were no lights showing and no response to the bell.

Nicola found the nearest pub. He wasn't there.

It struck her that the most likely place for him to go if he didn't want to be alone was to his club, particularly as it was a short walk from the Over-Seas League. She wouldn't be allowed to enter that masculine stronghold, but presumably they would give him a message. She took a taxi back to St James's Street.

The porter at the club shook his head in response to her query.

'Mr Russell isn't here at present, miss.'

'If he should come in later, could you tell him I was looking for him? I need to see him rather urgently.'

'If you'd care to write a message, miss, I'll see that Mr Russell gets it if he should come in this evening.'

From the club, Nicola returned to Richard's house in the hope that he might be there now. She hung about for half an hour and then scribbled another note.

Dear Richard,

I was so taken aback by your unexpected presence at the party that I don't think I made it clear what a wonderful surprise it was. Why did you leave early? I was going to ask you to join us for a post-party supper. I would like very much to iron out our misunderstandings and get back on our Istanbul footing. It's now nine forty-five p.m. and as you haven't come home yet, and are not at your club or the pub round the corner—I checked both—I'm going back to my place. Please call me.

Nicola.

She remembered Gina urging her to stick her neck out. After a moment's hesitation she added a postscript. 'I love you.'

Quickly she pushed the note through his letter-box before she could change her mind.

Then, for the fifth time that evening, she waved to a cruising taxi.

A familiar figure was pacing the pavement not far from her front door when the taxi turned into her street. There was no other traffic about and Richard heard the cab stopping and checked his stride to look back. When he saw Nicola climbing out he came hurrying towards her.

'I've been looking everywhere for you. How long have you been here?' she asked.

'Since I left the party. I have to talk to you.' He bent to speak to the driver. 'How much?'

'Four pounds, sir.'

'I have it here,' said Nicola, before Richard could pull out his wallet.

She handed the driver the fare and a tip. 'Thank you. Goodnight.'

Her smile at him was radiant. For Richard to be here had to mean Gina was right.

'I'm sorry you had to wait. Actually I was supposed to have supper with Gina and Margaret after the party, but I asked to be excused,' she said, handing him her latch-key. 'If only I'd come straight home you wouldn't have had this long wait.'

'It doesn't matter. You're here now.'

He unlocked the door and stood back for her to enter the hall. She turned on the light, time-switched to allow her to reach her own front door before it went out.

They went up the stairs without speaking and Richard, who still had her key-ring, unlocked the door at the top.

To hide her nervousness, she said, 'You must be longing to sit down. Let me fix you a drink.'

'What are you going to have?'

'A brandy and ginger, I think. I try not to mix grape and grain.'

'A brandy and ginger sounds great. This is a nice place you have here.' He moved towards the coffee-table and put her keys on it.

'It must seem poky compared with your house, but it's conveniently central and I like living at tree-top level.' She opened the fridge and took out a large bottle of chilled dry ginger and a tray of ice cubes.

'You've made it very comfortable...very personal. When I was here before I was in too much of a temper to take it in. I behaved very crassly that time...and have regretted it ever since.'

'You were entitled to be angry and I didn't handle it well.' She handed him his drink. 'Let's relax. It's been an exhausting day.'

They sat down at either end of her sofa. But Richard didn't lean back and stretch his long legs. He sat on the edge of the seat, his elbows on his knees and the glass held between them.

'I wondered if I'd ever come here again,' he said, glancing round at the bookshelves and pictures. 'After what happened last time, and then when you sent the rug back, it seemed unlikely.'

'I didn't send the rug back. I brought it in person. Didn't Jane Stonebridge tell you that?'

'She said a glamorous blonde in a hurry had dropped it off. It sounded as if you were on your way to a date. The fact that you returned it seemed quite significant. I knew you had liked it at Kas.'

'I loved it. I wanted to keep it. But how could I when you were furious with me?'

Richard put his untouched drink on the low table in front of him. Then he moved closer and took the glass from her hand. Holding both her hands in his, he said, 'I was angry because I had fallen in love with you. I wanted to tell you while we were in Istanbul. But I guess when you're thirty-four and you've never met the right girl and a lot of your friends have already been divorced from the wrong girl it makes caution seem a good idea. By the time we'd been apart a week, I was missing you badly. But a long-distance call is not the best way to tell a girl you love her, so I waited. And then of course when I got back the whole office was buzzing with the news about Trio.'

'Oh, Richard, if *only* I had told you before we left Istanbul. But you see, I thought if you loved me you would say so...and *then* I would tell you. When you didn't say what I wanted to hear, I was forced to conclude that on your side it was just a holiday affair.'

'I know. I must have been crazy. But I was only going to be away ten days and we'd known each other for two weeks—or so I thought. The irony of the situation is that when we arrived in Istanbul and something about you seemed familiar I thought it was because you were the girl I'd been waiting for all my life.'

'Yet the real first time you saw me I made no impression at all,' she said ruefully.

'Well, that's not surprising. I was preoccupied with the unpleasant task of sacking people. You were an unknown girl to whom I had to break some bad news. And you weren't the last on my hit-list,' he added. 'I had others to see after you.'

'How you must have hated it. You're such a kind person really. But I suppose you can't be kind if you're running a business.'

'Not if it's been mismanaged as badly as B & D before I took over. When things have been let go and are totally out of control, the remedies have to be drastic. But I didn't come here to talk about publishing. We have—or I hope we have—the rest of our lives to do that.' For the first time he smiled at her. 'What I want to discuss at the moment is a permanent merger of our private lives.'

# 4 FREE

## Romances and 2 FREE gifts just for you!

*You can enjoy all the heartwarming emotion of true love for FREE! Discover the heartbreak and happiness, the emotion and the tenderness of the modern relationships in Mills & Boon Romances.*

*We'll send you 4 Romances as a special offer from Mills & Boon Reader Service, along with the opportunity to have 6 captivating new Romances delivered to your door each month.*

**Claim your FREE books and gifts overleaf...**

# An irresistible offer from Mills & Boon

Become a regular reader of Romances with Mills & Boon Reader Service and we'll welcome you with 4 books, a CUDDLY TEDDY and a special MYSTERY GIFT all absolutely FREE.

And then look forward to receiving 6 brand new Romances each month, delivered to your door hot off the presses, postage and packing FREE! Plus our free Newsletter featuring author news, competitions, special offers and much more.

This invitation comes with no strings attached. You may cancel or suspend your subscription at any time, and still keep your free books and gifts.

It's so easy. Send no money now. Simply fill in the coupon below and post it to -
**Reader Service, FREEPOST, PO Box 236, Croydon, Surrey CR9 9EL.**

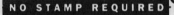

**NO STAMP REQUIRED**

# Free Books Coupon

**Yes!** Please rush me 4 FREE Romances and 2 FREE gifts! Please also reserve me a Reader Service subscription. If I decide to subscribe I can look forward to receiving 6 brand new Romances for just £10.80 each month, postage and packing FREE. If I decide not to subscribe I shall write to you within 10 days - I can keep the free books and gifts whatever I choose. I may cancel or suspend my subscription at any time. I am over 18 years of age.

Ms/Mrs/Miss/Mr _____ EP56I

Address _____

_____

Postcode _____ Signature _____

mps
MAILING
PREFERENCE
SERVICE

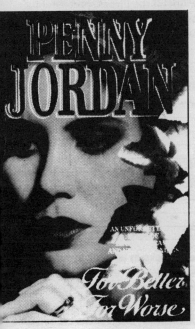

# Next Month's Romances

Each month you can choose from a wide variety of romance with Mills & Boon. Below are the new titles to look out for next month, why not ask either Mills & Boon Reader Service or your Newsagent to reserve you a copy of the titles you want to buy – just tick the titles you would like and either post to Reader Service or take it to any Newsagent and ask them to order your books.

*Please save me the following titles:*                    Please tick    ✓

| | | |
|---|---|---|
| HEART OF THE OUTBACK | Emma Darcy | |
| DARK FIRE | Robyn Donald | |
| SEPARATE ROOMS | Diana Hamilton | |
| GUILTY LOVE | Charlotte Lamb | |
| GAMBLE ON PASSION | Jacqueline Baird | |
| LAIR OF THE DRAGON | Catherine George | |
| SCENT OF BETRAYAL | Kathryn Ross | |
| A LOVE UNTAMED | Karen van der Zee | |
| TRIUMPH OF THE DAWN | Sophie Weston | |
| THE DARK EDGE OF LOVE | Sara Wood | |
| A PERFECT ARRANGEMENT | Kay Gregory | |
| RELUCTANT ENCHANTRESS | Lucy Keane | |
| DEVIL'S QUEST | Joanna Neil | |
| UNWILLING SURRENDER | Cathy Williams | |
| ALMOST AN ANGEL | Debbie Macomber | |
| THE MARRIAGE BRACELET | Rebecca Winters | |

If you would like to order these books in addition to your regular subscription from Mills & Boon Reader Service please send £1.90 per title to: Mills & Boon Reader Service, Freepost, P.O. Box 236, Croydon, Surrey, CR9 9EL, quote your Subscriber No:.................................... (If applicable) and complete the name and address details below. Alternatively, these books are available from many local Newsagents including W.H.Smith, J.Menzies, Martins and other paperback stockists from 12 March 1994.

Name:........................................................................................

Address:....................................................................................

......................................................Post Code:...........................

**To Retailer: If you would like to stock M&B books please contact your regular book/magazine wholesaler for details.**

You may be mailed with offers from other reputable companies as a result of this application.
If you would rather not take advantage of these opportunities please tick box ☐